Expert Witness: Wrongful Death

Judy Tarver

Carolynn,

To a great gal and
cat lover! Enjoy!

Judy

Other books by Judy Tarver:

Flight Plan to the Flight Deck:
Strategies for a Pilot Career

Published by PCS Publishing, Fort Worth, TX

ISBN – 978-0-9983333-0-4

Library of Congress Control Number: TXu001003617, date to be disclosed upon request.

Printed in the United States of America

Book Cover by Harry Howarth

Edited by Jan Howarth

This book is dedicated to my mom.

Acknowled

This book was a long time
been for the amazing sup
and coach, Samantha Sh
in the works. She is a g
characters and punching
story. And a special than
Dawson, who planted th
"You should write a boo

Thanks to my editor,
amazing and honest
husband, Harry, for the

I also appreciate my
members for trudging
it developed and pro
along the way.

Prologue

The small Benton Air turboprop carrying nine souls trudged its way through the murky clouds. The people on board were not aware that their fate was sealed.

"Give me a hand, Lou!" Captain Roger Daine struggled with the controls of the Beech 1900 aircraft. "Who the hell checked you out in training?"

Lou Jones attempted to open his mouth to respond, but his teeth were clenched together by an invisible vise. "I'm trying!" he finally spit out.

Daine interrupted. "Didn't you learn anything in class? I can't do everything myself here. This is a two-man job ..."

The luminous blue-violet glow of St. Elmo's fire shot across the windshield. The airplane, recognized for its reliable performance under the most adverse conditions, was being tested to its limits.

"We shouldn't be up in this mess. I hate flying in weather like this," Daine continued.

The weather on the approach to Chicago's O'Hare Airport was almost at "minimums"— the worst visibility conditions under which an aircraft may legally be flown. They had been holding for forty minutes waiting for air traffic control—ATC—to clear them for landing.

"This doesn't look good, Lou. We may have to divert. Get on the radio to dispatch again and get them to give us another alternate. Tell them we're close to bingo fuel."

Silence.

"Lou?"

"Huh?"

"Lou. Hello? Wake up! What do they think I am, a flight instructor? They don't pay me enough to train these new kids. Pimply-faced punks," Daine grumbled, as though he didn't think—or care—that Lou could hear him.

"How many hours do you have, kid?"

"Little over three hundred." Lou had just turned twenty-two. He was a decent pilot; he just needed seasoning.

"Shit, I might as well be alone." Daine took a sip of his coffee and then held the cup inches from Lou's face, his hand shaking. "Where did you get this coffee? It tastes like crap. Lousy stuff. Don't you listen? I said I like it black. Now I have heartburn."

The captain had a ruthless reputation for his demanding and condescending attitude, and he had earned it. When pilots bid for their flight schedules, they took great pains to avoid flying with him whenever possible. Lou, as low man on the seniority list, had ended up the loser again.

Lou wondered why Daine stayed with the commuter if he was so miserable. With his flight hours, he could be a major airline pilot. His lousy, arrogant attitude probably came out during interviews; none of the airlines would hire him.

"Well..." Lou hesitated, still at a loss for words. This was only his second trip with Benton Air, a small commuter airline based in Chicago. He didn't have much experience in bad weather, and had never encountered anything like this. There weren't many airlines he was qualified to work for. He didn't have enough hours yet for his airline transport pilot certification, and the FAA rules were pretty strict: pilots needed that certificate in order to fly any aircraft with more than nine seats. Plus, he needed one more birthday anyway; pilots had to be at least twenty-three.

"Well, what? Get on the horn and see what you can find out!"

Captain Daine had Lou frazzled. Lou compared Daine's attitude to the weather outside—bleak, nasty, and unforgiving. Lou's mind went blank as he fumbled with the dials.

The aircraft hit an air pocket, dropped with a jolt, and then leveled out, vibrating from the turbulent air mass. Passengers reached into the pockets attached to the seats in front of them and seized the airsick bags. As luck would have it, the airline provided an abundant supply. Those who weren't barfing were pale with fright, even the seasoned flyers.

Captain John Millingham, a check airman for Benton Air, sat in the first row of the passenger section, as the aircraft did not have a jump seat in the cockpit, and he had been furnished with a headset installed specifically for instructors and FAA inspectors through which he could listen to the cockpit crew. Dressed in his pilot's uniform, he was on his way to Chicago to fly a trip. The passengers looked at him for reassurance. He turned and smiled at the woman seated next to him. Her face was as white as the airsick bag she clutched.

In the cockpit, the pilots struggled to keep the aircraft smooth for the passengers.

Lou's eyes scanned the instrument panel. "Captain, the altimeter."

"What about it?" Daine's voice had lost its edge.

Lou looked at Daine. The captain's body, too large for the seat, dripped with sweat.

Even though the captain was a pain to work with, his experience and cool composure under pressure reassured the crew. If he looked nervous, they were in trouble.

Lou watched as the captain wiped his clammy hands on his sweat-soaked shirt and shook them vigorously.

"Are you okay, Captain?" he asked.

Daine's eyes darted at him, but before he could respond, his hands gravitated to his chest, and he let out a deep audible gasp. "Pain! I can't breathe!" He slumped over the controls.

"Oh my God! What ...!" Lou cried. "No! Not now!"

"John!" Lou shouted, knowing that his coworker sat in the back and could hear the conversation in the cockpit.

"What's going on up there?" John yelled. Not waiting for a response, he unbuckled his seatbelt and rushed into the cockpit, hanging on to whatever he could grasp to keep from falling as the airplane rocked. "What the hell ... is he dead?" John shouted as he took in the scene.

Lou didn't respond. He leaned over toward the captain, his head shifting from the instrument panel to the captain and back.

John squeezed into the cramped cockpit, grabbed the back of the captain's seat to steady himself, and tried to assist Lou in his efforts to pull the captain off the controls.

"Get back on the controls!" John cried. "Get this airplane level!" John turned and yelled into the cabin as he struggled to hold Daine back. "We need help up here! Is there a physician back there?"

Lou just stared, paralyzed with fear.

"What are you doing?" yelled John. "Pull up! Pull up!"

John let go of the seatback, held onto Daine with his left hand, grabbed the mike with his right, and pushed the button. "Mayday! Mayday!"

Chapter 1

Josey Cantwell hit the "Esc" key on the computer to end the PowerPoint presentation. "That's it for today. To sum it up, we are on the brink of a severe pilot shortage, and we need to get more creative and proactive. You can't build a pilot pool overnight. We've seen the number of qualified pilots dwindle for years, and until now no one would take responsibility. Everyone needs to step up to the plate. Many of you are starting to cancel flights because you can't fill your classes, and this is the tip of the iceberg. Thanks for your participation and great input. We will pick up on this next month back in DC."

Josey closed her computer just as Ed Murphy, her co-facilitator from the Federal Aviation Administration, approached her from the other side of the small, cramped room. "Who did you piss off this time, Josey?" Ed quipped, pointing to the brace on Josey's left hand. "Another scuffle with a renegade pilot? Every time I see you lately, you seem to have some part of your torso in a bandage."

"I wouldn't go there if I were you," Brad Smith said with a hint of humor in his voice.

Embarrassed by the inquiry, Josey felt a hot flash ascend up her neck to blend with her thick, curly red hair. She simply smiled, shrugged her shoulders, and changed the subject. "Thanks again for having the meeting in Fort Worth," she said to Ed. "It's a nice break from going to DC. I also wanted you to meet Brad since we just teamed up, and I need him to be in the loop on my projects."

Josey had just finished facilitating a meeting before an FAA rule-making committee. The topic dealt with the impending pilot shortage, minimum qualifications, and pilot selection methods and screening. There had been ten aviation representatives in attendance, and they were still in the room, many of them talking over what they had learned.

She looked up at Ed, a handsome guy, solidly built. At over six four he could never get lost in the crowd. "We had a good turnout," Josey said. "Just about every major and regional airline showed up this time. It's time they got their heads out of the sand. So far everyone knows there's a problem, but we're just now starting to get a grip on it. We can't put a Band-Aid on it and make it better. It's hitting the regional airlines and smaller commuter airlines right now, not to mention some of the large jet airlines, but before long the global and major airlines will be feeling the impact."

"We know that, and it will take a collaborative effort to solve it," Ed said.

The conversation paused as an attractive, middle-aged woman walked up.

"Josey," said Ed, "this is Claudette Floyd. She's representing a group of investors for a start-up airline. She's new in the industry, and this is her first meeting."

"Sorry I came in late," Claudette said. "I'm glad to finally meet you in person. I hear you're the expert in this arena. Those statistics really struck a chord with me—an eye-opener for sure. We're concerned we won't be able to gear up by our deadline because we can't find enough pilots who'll accept our pay and benefit packages. The competition among the airlines is stiff."

"I hear you," said Josey. "You have your work cut out for you. Glad it's not me. This storm's been brewing for a long time."

"How did you end up in a career like this?" Claudette asked.

"It just happened," explained Josey. "I started

out as a temp in human resources and loved helping people get hired. My husband, Pete, was a pilot, so it was only fitting that I ended up doing something with pilots. Over the years I had an opportunity to interview thousands of pilots and couldn't help but learn something. Honestly, I didn't like the politics of the big corporations, so I ended up as a consultant.

"For someone who is not a pilot, Josey understands pilots more than anyone I know," Ed added.

"Well, I did fly an F-4 Phantom once—" Josey stopped speaking when Brad's phone rang.

"Excuse me a second. This might be important." Brad walked to an empty corner of the room to get some privacy.

Josey watched him as he continued his conversation. He looked agitated. He ended the call and walked back, the twinkle in his eyes gone. He ran his hand through his thick hair, a habit he had when he was perplexed. "There's been another crash," he said. "A Benton Air turboprop just went down in the lake near Chicago—eight passengers and three crew members. They don't believe there were any survivors."

"Damn." Josey, ignoring the others, walked over to the window and stared outside.

The impending storm brewing in the west and headed their way caused a premature darkening of the dusky-gray afternoon sky. The weather report called for possible tornadoes.

Brad and the others followed her. "Controllers said they heard a Mayday and then lost communication with the pilots before the plane crashed," Brad continued. "Mayday only. They can't figure it out. Then nothing."

"This is the last thing we need," Josey said. "Another major crash so soon—three commuter airlines within the last three months. First there was the Cloudair crash in Florida, then Orleans Air Cargo in Lake Pontchartrain near New Orleans. Now Benton Air. The media will have a field day with this. Did you get any feedback on a possible cause?"

"No, that's it," Brad replied. His voice carried through the small room. The attendees stopped in their tracks, and the room became silent, with the exception of an escalating clicking noise. Brad reached over and pulled the pen out of Josey's hand. She looked at him with a blank stare until she realized what she had been doing and that everyone was staring at her. "Josey, they might need us on the case."

She nodded.

Once Josey and Brad regained their composure, the rest of the group gathered their belongings and left.

"This has been one long day. I'm glad it's over." Josey looked stoic in her standard black pants and long, black tunic top. Out of habit, she gently rubbed the charm on her necklace—a tiny gold replica of an F-4 Phantom set against a disk of sodalite, a beautiful blue stone with a white matrix that gives the appearance of a cloud-filled sky. The stone is also known for its healing and mental focus properties.

"Come on, Brad," she said. "Give me a hand." Encumbered by the brace on her left hand, she managed a valiant attempt at putting an overwhelming mound of documents into an already overstuffed briefcase.

"Could they have crammed any more people into this little room?" she asked. The small mahogany table riddled with dents from excessive use and littered with stacks of documents was designed to accommodate six to eight people and took up most of the conference room.

She saw Brad watching as she straightened her necklace. He had given it to her the year before for her birthday, and she always wore it whenever they were together.

"You seem a little pale today, Josey," Brad said. "Are you sure you're okay? You really need more rest after that close call last week."

"I can't believe there's been another crash," she said, ignoring his remarks. "We're still deep into the Cloudair crash in Florida. I'm anxious to get the analysis of the cockpit voice recorder. That should help. I reviewed the copilot's credentials. He was new, just out of training. He only had three hundred and fifty hours of multi-engine experience and less than eight hundred total. The captain had been there a long time and had over seven thousand hours in the aircraft."

"I wish they had the new solid-state digital black boxes installed," Brad said. "The one in that aircraft recorded for only thirty minutes, and then started over."

"Okay, Brad. Enough business for now," Josey said. "And there goes my vacation!"

Brad grabbed her briefcase, and they walked out of the building together. "Josey, you have to relax—I'm reading a nine out of ten on your stressometer."

"Stessometer? Did you just invent that? I guess you're right," she said, hating to admit that Brad could read her so well.

"Of course I'm right. When was the last time you actually got away?" He laughed as they headed to the parking lot.

"Oh, I guess the same time you did. Remember that conference in Orlando right after you came back into town?

"Well, the doctor said you should take it easy. Your EKG was abnormal, and we don't want you having a heart attack."

"Look, it's fine. Just one of those normal, abnormal occurrences. No need for worry."

Brad rolled his eyes as he opened the passenger door of his vintage 1963 Mercedes Benz—his pride and joy. The paint was the original graphite gray. Also original were the tan leather seats and burl wood dash. The exterior and interior still sported the original features of the car; the rest of the car was state-of-the art new.

"Let's go, Josephine, before it starts to hail," Brad said as he looked up at the dark sky and a large drop of water splatted right in the middle of his forehead.

Friday afternoon Fort Worth traffic loomed ahead, and the exhausted couple yearned for the upcoming weekend—weather permitting.

She threw him a rebuking glance. "Call me Josephine one more time, and I'll dent your precious car." The name had been handed down to her from her paternal grandmother. She had adored both of her grandmothers, whose exciting Irish and Scottish backgrounds were tightly woven into Josey's personality, but she'd always thought the names were outdated. The shortened version suited her just fine.

"Hey, no need to get huffy. I'm just playing with you. Don't hurt my car."

Josey had known Brad since she was nineteen years old. He had been her husband Pete's best friend at Texas A&M and the best man at their wedding. Brad and Pete had gone their separate ways after college—Pete joined the Marines as an F-4 Phantom fighter pilot, and Brad went the army route as a fixed-wing and helicopter pilot. When her husband was lost over North Korea a few years into his service, Brad moved on to the CIA, always hoping he would one day find Pete. Years passed, and he retired from the Company. He had recently moved back to Texas to work with Josey as a consultant with the NTSB and other aviation-related organizations, both government and commercial.

"You've always cared more about this car of yours than you have about anyone," Josey said, blowing off his attempt to chide her. She laughed back at him, her thick, curly hair already starting to frizz from the dampness.

"She is the only wife I've ever had. You were already taken. And, look, you're still wearing your wedding ring."

She looked at her finger. "Well ... anyway ... I'm sure you say that to all the women." Josey wouldn't admit it, but she loved his car almost as much as he did. Even though it was old, it was still the most elegant car she'd ever ridden in. The luxurious, soft leather seats molded to her body, and the ride was so smooth she felt as if she was floating down the road.

Brad dropped Josey off at her house, barely slowing down to let her out so he could get his car to shelter. He lived just a few miles from Josey's house in an upscale townhouse community.

"Don't forget, we need to look at office space this weekend," he said.

"Yeah, yeah. Like working with you full time is going to lower my stress level."

Brad saluted and drove off.

Chapter 2

Josey raced from Brad's car and landed on her front porch just before the torrential rain fell. As she entered her sprawling, four-bedroom brick house in a suburb near the Dallas/Fort Worth International Airport, her orange-and-white tabby cat, Luc, greeted her, purring and rubbing gently against her legs. She took a deep breath of the soothing scent of vanilla that always lingered throughout the cheerful rooms.

"Coffee. I need coffee. I'm so addicted," she told the cat. She went straight to the kitchen and set her computer bag on the floor and her purse on the counter. She turned on her espresso machine, took some half and half from the fridge, and put it into her electric frother.

While waiting for the coffee machine to heat up, she glanced at her cellphone and realized she had several missed calls and two messages. Before listening to any messages, she flipped through the caller ID numbers: Rene, her daughter; Cary, Rene's twin brother;

unknown; and Brad. There were two actual messages. She tapped on the first number and put it on speaker. "Ms. Cantwell, this is Tony McIntyre, legal counsel for Viscount Air Transport. We would like to retain you as an expert witness for a lawsuit against our company. It is time sensitive, so if you could return my call as soon as possible, we would be ever so grateful." McIntyre closed his message by reciting his contact information.

"Ever so grateful? Sheesh." She was familiar with Viscount. The company operated an on-demand charter and cargo operation that flew DC-8s and L-382s in and out of depressed areas around the world. The DC-8s were used primarily for passenger charter trips. The L-382s were the civilian version of the military C-130s and were used for cargo because of their rugged versatility and their capability to operate from short, rough dirt strips.

Brad thought they ran a sleazy operation. He actually sometimes did covert work to gather information on the company for some government agencies, although no one would ever admit it publicly. Most of Viscount's pilots were cowboys and rogues, ready and willing to go just about anywhere and transport just about anything. Josey had heard that the pilots had been trying to bargain for hazard pay when they flew into dangerous areas. But the company held out, not wanting to admit that the pilots were put in life-threatening situations.

She glanced at the picture hanging on the wall near the counter—there wasn't a nook or cranny in the house that didn't have a family picture strategically placed, along with a large collection of crosses she had collected over the years. Pete and the twins were standing with her in front of an F-4 Phantom. She stood proud and straight, wearing the Marine flight suit given to her for her demo flight in the backseat of the aircraft. Pete had let her fly it for a few seconds, thus her claim to having flown the F-4.

But now looking at the picture only made her recall the day in 1989 when the Marine colonel had come to her house to tell her that Pete had gone missing in action over North Korea. They never found the aircraft or the two crew members, but Josey had never given up faith, and her faith was the only thing that kept her grounded. She grabbed her small, pink diary—one of several—that had been sitting next to the phone and jotted a note to Pete, still trying to keep his spirit alive. "Pete, I know you will be happy that Brad is back and working with me. I just hope we can click. You know how different we are. Brad is such an unorganized free spirit, and you know I'm a control freak. Fingers crossed. Brad has always been there for me since you disappeared. I'm glad he is here, and so are the kids."

Speaking of Brad, Josey realized she hadn't listened to his message, so she tapped on his name. "Hey, Josey, I need you to do me a favor. An old friend of mine is in town and needs a place to crash for a while. I told her she could stay in your garage apartment. She'll help you out around the house. Expect her soon."

"What? That was fast. I just left him!" Just as she hit the delete button, the doorbell rang.

Chapter 3

Josey opened the door. It took her several seconds to focus. When Brad had said "old," she'd thought he was referring to his history with this person. Facing her was a short, wiry woman, maybe in her early seventies, standing straight as a rail. She held a cigarette in her right hand. She cradled a scary-looking Pomeranian dog under her left arm while managing to hold a dripping umbrella. A nondescript bag lay at her feet. Her hair was hidden by a dark-brown beret. Her clothes looked like throwbacks from the sixties' hippie era—not the happy, flowing costumes of the flower children, but the dark turtlenecks of the brooding poets who sat in the corners of the cabarets smoking cigarettes and drinking coffee while listening to folk songs like "Hang Down your Head Tom Dooley." She wore dark-rimmed glasses that took up most of her face and made her eyes look three times their normal size. But the real attention grabber was the large gold amulet hanging around her neck on a thin leather chord. An intricate design that Josey couldn't decipher surrounded a luminous stone. As the woman moved, the color seemed to change from blue to green depending on the angle.

Holy shit! Josey thought, trying to maintain her composure. She forgot all about the coffee.

The woman interrupted Josey's trance. "Brad send me. I cook for you. Go pay driver." She handed Josey her umbrella.

"Huh?" Josey looked outside and saw the taxi driver standing in front of the cab. The downpour had subsided into a soft drizzle.

Still trying to process everything, she rushed over to the counter and grabbed her purse. Still holding the umbrella, she went outside to pay the driver. "How much?"

"A hundred seventy-five."

"You've got to be kidding! Where did she come from? Oh, never mind. I don't think I want to know." She paid the driver and hurried back to the house. Her guests were still standing in the doorway. As she approached the door, she noticed Luc hissing at the dog, who was growling back, baring sharp, white teeth.

"Come in."

"Of course."

"What is your name?

"Natasha."

"Of course it is," Josey said under her breath. "Where are you from?"

Natasha ignored the question. "Show me room."

Josey didn't know what to make of this. Maybe Russian? Or at least from somewhere around there? The woman and her dog were creepy. "Sure. There's a nice apartment over the garage. You'll have your own privacy since the garage is detached from the house."

"Of course."

Josey noticed she had only one large cloth satchel. "Let me help. Is that your only luggage?"

"The rest comes later."

Josey took Natasha to the efficiency apartment that had been there when she bought the house. The kids had played there when they were little, and her friends and relatives usually stayed there when they came to visit. A nice amenity.

Natasha looked around the friendly room. "This will work."

"Okay then. I'll let you get settled, and we can talk later. I hope you don't mind, but I would appreciate it if you wouldn't smoke in the house."

"Of course."

By the way, what is your dog's name?

"Boris."

Of course, Josey thought while resisting the urge to roll her eyes. Brad had some explaining to do.

There was a covered breezeway between the house and the garage, so Josey did not need to worry about the rain. She walked back to the house and opened the curtains in the kitchen and living room to let in the last of the light as the storm picked up steam again. Quarter-sized hail began to fall, pinging on the ground and bouncing up into the air. Tornado warnings were still in effect.

She looked at Luc and said with a hint of sarcasm, "Hope Brad got his precious car inside before it got pounded."

She went back to the kitchen, whipped up an espresso, and went into her office. After kicking her shoes off under the desk, she felt around for the small wooden foot massager among the pile of shoes previously deposited in the hollow space. She rubbed her feet on the wooden balls.

She spotted an empty space on the desk and pulled out a notepad. She glanced up at the clock sitting on a shelf next to her desk amid a myriad of pictures of two teeny toddlers frolicking with their grandma, granddad, and Pete. The hands of the clock were perpendicular—six o'clock on the dot.

Although starving, she decided to make the call to Tony McIntyre at Viscount Air Transport first, hoping he would still be in the office. She grabbed a pencil and dialed his number.

Tony answered his own phone right away. "Ms. Cantwell, thank you for calling back so fast. You were referred to us by Larry Townsend, executive director of the Airline Legal Resource Center. He says you're an expert in evaluating pilot credentials. We need your help."

"I appreciate your call, Tony, but I'm really wrapped up in some exhaustive work right now—"

He interrupted. "This shouldn't be too time consuming. Just review some documents and give us your opinion. Maybe a deposition. But hopefully we can settle this without going to trial. You were highly recommended, and we want to get through this as quickly as possible to avoid any unnecessary publicity."

"Well, give me the background, and I'll see if it's something I can do," Josey said with an audible sigh.

Tony began. "Annie Cisco, the wife of one of our employees, Bobby Cisco, is suing our company. He recently died in a small airplane crash in Louisiana. She said that he was on his way back to work when the accident happened. Annie claims the company placed undue pressure on Bobby to get to work, and he took an unnecessary risk by attempting to fly back in bad weather. She insists that Bobby told her the company constantly forced the pilots to push the limits of their responsibilities, not giving them enough rest time between flights and coercing them to take trips on their days off."

"Is that true?" Josey asked, finally getting a chance to speak. She remembered what Brad and other pilots had told her.

"Of course not. But we run a tight ship here." Tony's tone at first fringed on indignant, but he quickly softened his manner.

Josey figured he didn't want to turn her off because he needed her help. He seemed to be making a conscious effort to schmooze her.

Tony moved on. "Anyway, she's suing Viscount for wrongful death and is claiming that, if not for this accident, the company promised to promote him to copilot, and eventually he would reach his goal to fly for a major airline. According to her, he had built up a sufficient amount of time on the side to enhance his career opportunities." Tony took an audible deep breath. "To be honest, Bobby wasn't well liked around here. He was pushy and self-serving. We were in the process of finding a replacement, but people with his dual qualifications are hard to come by." He paused. "Mrs. Cantwell—"

"Please, call me Josey."

"Josey, we need you to take a look at the documents we've been able to retrieve—flight records and transcripts from the depositions given by the witnesses for the plaintiff and defense. We need your expert opinion on what Bobby's career opportunities really were. We need to know what you think the odds were that he'd actually become a pilot for a major airline."

The case didn't sound too complicated—just review a few documents and probably write up a report on her opinion.

Although her plate was full, Josey replied,

"Okay. I'll take a look at what you have and let you know what I think. But I need to let you know that I'm committed to work on an NTSB investigation, and it will take priority if they need me." Josey didn't mention anything relating to the Benton Air crash.

"That's not a problem. I'm sure we can work around your schedule." He almost crooned the response.

Tony paused as though he was working up the courage for something, and then added. "Here's the kicker. We would have given more notice, but we just found out about you. We're scheduled to depose Annie in Memphis on Monday, and I'd like you to sit in on the deposition."

She looked at her calendar—Friday already. Most of the days were already blocked out for the next week. "You're in luck. So far, I'm free on Monday. Send me the documents right away, but I'm not sure I'll be able to get much done before then."

"I understand. Hopefully you'll get a good feel for the case during the deposition, and we can discuss it on the airplane." Tony sounded relieved, but with a hint of "I just connived my way around you." He continued, "Can you e-mail or fax me a copy of your curriculum vitae and your fee schedule—you know ... the formalities? They say you are the go-to person in these types of cases. Again, ever so grateful."

"I'll send the documents right over," Josey said.

"Thanks. Okay, I'll get our documents to you right away. Again, don't worry about getting it done this weekend. See you on Monday morning. Eight fifteen at the Viscount ticket counter," Tony replied.

"Look for the woman with the bright red hair wearing a black outfit and a necklace with an F-4 on it," Josey said just before he hung up.

—✦—

Tony hung up, looked over the desk at Royce Allemand, vice president of international operations, and smirked. "Got her. It's in the bag."

"Good. We need to get this case resolved right away. Try to keep it as low-key as possible. We don't need more negative publicity. Whoever this lady is, I hope she can find a way to get us off the radar."

Josey sighed. She'd done it again. "I don't have a good feeling about this," she said to the cat. "Can't pinpoint it." There was something in Tony's tone that worried her. Maybe the rumors were true, and if so, she didn't want to get wrapped up in something underhanded. "Why can't I ever say no? Oh well, the pay is good. I want to buy a new patio set for my deck—if I ever get time to enjoy it." She rambled on as she glanced down at Luc. His little head tilted up as though he understood exactly what she'd said.

"Let's eat, Luc. Spaghetti's sounding pretty darn good right now, don't you think? Let's see if Brad wants to join us. Maybe he can shed some light on Natasha."

She was glad Brad was in town full time now. She reached up and grabbed a small picture of her wedding day. Brad was standing next to Pete, both in their Sunday best. Brad reminded her of Clark Kent, Superman's alter ego—well actually maybe Superman himself. He was her hero. A little over six feet tall, he had deep blue-green eyes with eyelashes a girl only dreams of. Even today his thick black hair fell just below his ears, adding a hint of carefree charm. The aging process was starting to take its toll. The hair had a touch of silver in just the right areas, but he accepted it with grace and a sense of humor.

He had a colorful and eclectic past. If she hadn't known him already, she would have wondered if his name was really Smith. He had continued his covert employment until his recent "retirement." At least he claimed to be finished, except for his work with the NTSB—and now as her new partner.

The storm was severe, so Brad opted to stay home. Josey did not see Natasha again that evening.

Chapter 4

A private courier arrived at Josey's house early Saturday morning with a large package from Viscount. She signed for documents and went back to her office to review the files.

She read the cover letter. It confirmed the location of the deposition—downtown Memphis. After the accident, Annie and her son had moved back there and were staying with her parents.

Arrangements had been made for her to spend the night at the Peabody Hotel, one of Josey's favorites. She loved watching the famous trained mallard ducks waddling through the lobby.

"They say that Cisco fellow led the life of an entitled charlatan, but you can't help feeling sorry for the wife and kid," Josey mumbled, shifting in her chair as Luc tried to squeeze in next to her.

Rene slipped into the room unannounced. Rene worked full-time for her mother as an administrative assistant, her role often expanding according to Josey's particular needs. She lived only a few miles away with her husband, Adam, and three-year old son, Matt, in a new development that was occupied mostly by young professionals. There were lots of young children for Matt to play with.

"Charlatan? Is that one of your fancy words for the day? Why don't you just say jerk?"

"I'm not totally vocabulary challenged, you know," Josey retorted as she turned to acknowledge Rene's appearance. "I like that word—charlatan."

It was common for Josey and Rene to joke around. Rene respected her mom and knew how far she could go with her wisecracks.

Josey didn't expect Rene to work on Saturdays, and she wasn't much in the mood to work either.

"Why did you take on another case?" Rene asked. "Your schedule is already maxed out. How do you expect to find the time to do the work if you want any social life at all?"

"I know, I know. But it seems like a pretty easy case. However, I do have to learn to say no." Josey continued, "You know, I hate these kinds of cases—testifying against someone who lost a spouse ... having to face them at a trial." She stacked up some of the files she'd been looking at. "Talking to the lawyer brought back memories. His company flies C-130s. I'm still mad at Cary for taking us on that airplane ride in his C-130 and trying to scare the bejesus out of us. I think he flew through that storm on purpose." She was proud of her son. He was in the Texas Air National Guard while he worked full-time as an engineer at a local aerospace corporation.

"I thought it was fun."

"Well, getting hit by lightning isn't fun."

"Like Cary said, 'You're just a chicken. That airplane can fly through a hurricane.'" She laughed. "Okay, back to reality, Mom. Almost everything you do these days deals with death. Those airplane accidents ... all those wrongful death cases. It's morose! You need a break. Haven't you had enough? That last psycho you testified against attacked you and tried to burn down the house. Come on, Mom. You are so lucky Brad showed up when he did. You can't always count on him being there just in the nick of time." She looked at Josey's left arm and hand, still in the brace from the fiasco.

"I did not see that coming. That was an age discrimination case. He was just looking for an easy buck. There was no clear evidence that anyone discriminated against him. But I guess graceful losing wasn't his strength, especially when he was suing for a couple million."

"That's an understatement," Rene said.

"Okay, okay. This will be my last one for a while."

"You say that, but I'll believe it when I see it."

"Change the subject, okay? I get enough grief from Cary. I don't need you harping on me too." These lectures from her children and her friends were starting to get on her nerves. But they were right. It was time to stop. Josey really wasn't sure what drove her to keep going on like that—it wasn't the money.

"Look," said Rene, "I don't know how it happens, but the shit always seems to hit the fan when you get involved."

Josey was about to change the subject when, somehow, out of nowhere, appeared Natasha. "Breakfast is ready. Now eat."

Josey and Rene exchanged confused glances.

"Where? How? Breakfast?" Josey couldn't spit it out.

"I fix good breakfast. Go eat." Natasha looked at Rene. "You too. You are too skinny."

"Rene, this is Natasha. Brad sent her."

Josey and a puzzled Rene walked into the kitchen. On the counter sat a beautiful mushroom quiche along with a plate full of sausages and bacon.

"How did you do this?" asked Josey.

"Is easy."

"Well then, let's eat! I need to get back to work."

They ate in silence until Natasha suddenly disappeared as quickly as she had appeared.

The breakfast was unbelievable. Josey wondered where Natasha had learned to cook.

"What was that all about? Who is Natasha? How long will she be here?" Rene asked.

"I'm still not sure. Brad asked if she could stay here. I haven't talked to him yet. I'm still trying to process it."

"She's creepy."

"You took the words right out of my mouth. You haven't seen the dog yet."

"The dog?"

"Later. Back to work. Would you set up these files for me when you come in on Monday?"

"Sure, no problem. I'll have everything in tip-top shape when you get back," Rene said. "So you can mess it back up again," she said under her breath.

"I heard that."

Josey studied Rene for a moment. While their familial relationship was obvious, her daughter was much taller—about five-foot-ten—and had long, fine medium-blond hair, usually pulled back in a ponytail. Little Matt placed number one on her list of priorities. This job gave her a chance to spend more time with him.

"I still don't get it," said Rene, continuing a persistent theme. "You don't have to work this hard. I know I ask this all the time, but remind me—why do you do it? It's as if you're on a crusade to make sure companies hire the best pilots out there. Don't you think they know what they're doing?"

"Sure they do. I keep reminding myself to leave it be, but you know how it all started."

"Again, remind me." Rene sat on the arm of

the chair that stood next to the desk.

"I know I told you this, but you were little when it happened. Back when I first got started in the pilot hiring business, we had an applicant who failed the MMPI—the Minnesota Multiphasic Personality Inventory. Simply put, the test looks for deviant characteristics. One of my best friends, a management pilot, had flown with the guy in the military. Because my friend had a pretty high-level job over there, he learned that his friend had failed the test and talked me into giving it to him again. I did, and he failed the second time. Again my friend put pressure on me to move him on in the process. Against my better judgment, I did. Turned out the guy was a psycho. He went nuts on a flight one day and tried to take the controls from the captain. No one really knows why. Luckily, the captain was able to overpower him and land the aircraft safely. Even though I wasn't punished for it, I never forgot, and to this day, I go above and beyond never to make a mistake like that again." Josey could feel a warm flush moving up her neck.

"I understand, Mom, but it turned out okay. People make mistakes. You can't keep dwelling on the past. That was a long time ago, and I'm sure you have more than made up for it over the years. It's time to slow down."

"I know. But the outcome could have been disastrous. I wish you hadn't asked. I'm so embarrassed about it. I know I need to work on letting it go."

"On another note, you are really lucky to have me here—no one else would put up with your mess. You wouldn't be able to find anything without me. Plus you have a built-in cat sitter," Rene added as she straightened up some stacks of books littering the bookcase, careful not to disturb the last picture they had of her dad.

"Are you fishing for a raise?" Josey laughed.

"Are you biting? I have to go. See ya later!" Rene kissed her mother and headed out the door.

"See ya!"

Josey's mind redirected to the case at hand, and she turned to the cat. "I'll take a look at the documents and see if the guy actually had a future outside Viscount." She looked at the stack of interrogatories, depositions, and exhibits. "Well, Luc. Help me out here. Where do I start?" She groaned as the cat jumped from the chair and curled up on the big pillow next to her desk.

Josey flipped through the documents to get a feel for the content. The quick once-over told

her that she had a lot of work to do. Open-
and shut-cases just didn't exist; regret was
already setting in.

Chapter 5

Josey arrived at the airport early Monday morning. She was glad the weather had finally cleared up. Luckily, the storms over the weekend had caused little damage. The airport was bustling with Monday-morning business travelers walking briskly as they talked on the phone or texted busily. She thought about how casual travelers had become over the years, and she missed the old days when traveling was a privilege and people were polite and excited about their journeys.

It wasn't hard to pick out Tony at the ticket counter. He was the only person dressed in a suit and carrying the standard lawyer's bulky briefcase—the kind that looked like a pilot's flight bag only without the aviation and union stickers covering the sides.

Aside from the legal look, he appeared nothing as she had expected after hearing his deep, slow Southern drawl on the phone. She had envisioned a tall, husky, youngish guy, and he wasn't much taller than she. He was slim and wiry like a runner, with thinning gray hair.

He was good looking, and his clothes were impeccably tailored. Josey wasn't much into fashion, but she could tell that his clothes were expensive. She glanced down at her basic black pantsuit and felt less than chic, but just as quickly tossed the feeling aside.

Tony spotted Josey, waved, and started walking her way.

"Josey?" He held out his hand. "I'm awfully glad you could make it. Sorry we couldn't give you more notice, but I can use the time on the airplane to brief you more."

"I have to admit I didn't get much reviewed over the weekend. The family already had plans. But I'll be sure to go through the documents this week and get something back to you by Friday," Josey replied.

She saw him glance at her left arm and was waiting for the next question, but the boarding call saved her again from questions she preferred not to answer.

Viscount had sprung for first class, a pleasant surprise. Josey loved traveling first class. The cabin was full of Monday-morning business passengers.

"Tell me more about the case," Josey said as they buckled up for takeoff.

Josey grabbed the cup of coffee offered by the flight attendant and pulled out a little notepad.

Tony started. "Well, Bobby was employed with us as a flight engineer and mechanic. However, we have no record that Bobby was ever scheduled to work that day. Annie said that Bobby called her that morning, right before he left Vicksburg, Mississippi, and told her to make sure his uniform was ready—that he was on his way home.

"Our investigation actually did reveal that a call had been placed to his cell phone from Viscount that morning, but nobody will own up to calling him. We think it might have been a prank. There are lots of Viscount people who didn't like Bobby. We're still trying to figure it out.

"She also said that he told her the company was promising to upgrade him to copilot, and it was just a matter of time until he started school in the DC-8. We have no record of that either, although we know he was constantly badgering the chief pilot and the manager of the HR department to give him an interview. Like I said, Bobby wasn't very popular, but the fact is, his current flight engineer slash mechanic skills were more important to us.

"The FAA investigation is ongoing; however, so far they haven't discovered anything that would lead them to believe that it was anything but an accident—pilot error. The weather was bad. They think Cisco got disoriented, lost control, and crashed into the trees."

Tony kept going. "Seems Annie wasn't the only one who thought he was heading home for work. Some lady called the FAA after she heard about the crash on TV. They said she was hysterical ... acted as if she was a close friend. She confirmed the story. Said she drove him back to the airport so he could get back to work. She said he was really upset. She mentioned a guy named Claude who was fueling the aircraft. But we haven't had a chance to talk to him. The regular guy, Steve, was out. Apparently he's somewhat of a vagrant. Comes and goes. Nobody has been able to find him yet. Funny, nobody at the airport knew this Claude fellow. He hasn't shown up again either."

As Josey listened to Tony, she continued to have that uneasy feeling. He was all professional but polite in a slightly condescending way. He wasn't succeeding in his attempts to make her like him. Regardless, he seemed to have a good grasp of the case.

"I'm a pilot myself," Tony mentioned as he puffed out his chest. "Mostly single-engine fun flying, but it does make it easier when I'm involved in cases like this one."

"I'm not a pilot," Josey said, "but after years of working with pilots, I know the lingo. I've never had the interest or the aptitude."

They made small talk during the rest of the flight, and Josey took some time to read over several of the documents. She soon noticed that the plane was taxiing to the terminal. "Don't tell anyone," she said to Tony, "but I'm afraid to fly. Thanks for the good conversation. I didn't even notice the takeoff and landing—those are the parts I really hate."

Neither Josey nor Tony had checked any baggage, so they went quickly through the terminal to the taxi stand. They hopped into the cab and arrived at the law offices of Mitchell, McGee and Smiley ten minutes early for their meeting. The firm occupied a suite of offices in a small business complex in downtown Memphis.

Upon their arrival, the receptionist escorted Josey and Tony into an elegant conference room that was decked out in upscale Texas décor—an odd touch in Tennessee. The conference table—solid, glossy, standard mahogany—could seat at least fourteen people.

"That coffee smells good; I hope they have plenty," Josey said as she glanced around and noted a buffet set up along the wall with an assortment of coffee, hot water for tea, and ice water. Fancy china, Josey thought. This is an upscale law firm.

The court reporter was setting up her shorthand machine and a laptop.

Cal Mitchell, Annie Cisco's lawyer, walked over to greet them. "Good morning," he started. "I'm Cal. Everyone is here, and we're ready to start. Please have a seat on this side of the table." He pointed to the coffee setup. "Help yourself to a beverage." Josey hadn't waited for the invitation; she already had a cup in hand.

Seems pleasant enough, Josey thought. Cal's husky body matched Tony's voice. But that was the extent of the similarity. Appearing to be in his late forties, Cal was somewhat disheveled, his wavy, black hair totally uncontrollable. He had a heavy accent that Josey recognized from visits to her grandparent's home in Baltimore when she was growing up. He was wearing "business chic"—blue jeans and brown snakeskin cowboy boots, a feeble attempt to shed his East Coast identity. Josey also noticed the small hole minus the earring in his left ear. Definitely not the conservative lawyer when he was off duty, she thought.

Annie Cisco, looking out of place in this setting, sat quietly at the table. She was not wearing any makeup, and her simple, blue A-line dress looked homemade. Her black shoes needed polishing, and the faux leather on the small heels was torn from the soles in several places.

Annie stood when Josey came over to introduce herself before she settled into her own seat on the other side of the table.

"I'm terribly sorry about your loss," Josey said with sincere empathy.

"Thank you" was all Annie said.

Annie was petite and frail. Her light-brown hair was cut just below her ears and fell in soft curls around her face. It was hard to believe that she'd been married to Bobby who, Josey had been told, had been outgoing and gregarious.

The court reporter sat at the end of the table. The two adversary legal teams sat on opposite sides of the table with Annie on one side of the court reporter and Tony on the other side. Cal sat next to Annie. A young lady, probably a paralegal, was seated on the other side of Cal.

The court reporter introduced herself as Jennifer March. The two lawyers handed her their business cards to make it easier for her to record their information into the transcript.

Jennifer started the session. "Mrs. Cisco, please raise your right hand." When Annie was ready, she continued, "Do you swear to tell the truth, the whole truth and nothing but the truth?"

"Yes," Annie said, her voice barely audible.

Tony began in his slow Texas drawl. "Annie, as a courtesy to Ms. March, could you please be sure to answer each question clearly and try to not shake your head yes or no. The transcripts must plainly state your answer. I notice that you speak softly. You're going to have to try to speak up. If you have any problem understanding my questions, please be sure to say so.

"Okay."

"Then, let's get started. Please state your full name for the record."

"Ann Sims-Cisco."

Tony asked the standard preliminary questions such as address and where she worked.

Josey was unnerved by Tony's style. He was slightly condescending without being confrontational, but she could tell Annie was uneasy.

Tony continued, "Mrs. Cisco. I know this is difficult for you. I'll try to make it quick and simple." Annie nodded, and he asked his first question: "How long were you and Mr. Cisco married?"

"Eleven years."

"Do you have any children?"

"A boy, Robert."

"I noticed all of the documents refer to your husband as Bobby. Is that his given name? Is Robert a second?"

"No, Bobby's parents gave him the name Bobby. He hated it. It seemed so childish to him. That's why he named our son Robert— and that's what we call him."

"Tell me a little about your husband's background—a little history, going over his past employment."

Cal interrupted, "Question is too broad."

"Okay, I can just ask year by year about Bobby's career path, or she can just give me an overview." Tony's voice had a hint of sarcasm.

Annie started talking: "Well, Bobby grew up in Texas. I guess he wasn't much into higher education back then, so when he graduated from high school, he joined the navy. I met him right after he enlisted when he was in his technical training as an ... uh, aviation electrician at the base in Millington. I was living nearby, outside Memphis. We didn't date long. In fact, we fell in love right away, and were married within a month."

Annie sighed and stared into space for a while. Her eyes scanned the room. Everyone was staring at her, waiting patiently. She turned bright red. "Sorry, I'm getting off base here. Anyway, his first assignment was at the naval air station in Dallas where he worked on the A-4 aircraft. Uh ... we were there for four years. Then he was transferred to NAS Moffett Field just outside of San Jose, California. He worked on ... let me think ... it had four engines, but wasn't a jet. Hold on, I should know this. Wait, I remember—a P-3. Did something with seaplane patrol or something. Then he got out and went to work for Viscount. He was a mechanic and flight engineer there." Annie spoke as though she was sedated—staring ahead, rambling as if she had the information memorized. Josey felt sorry for her.

Tony continued his questioning. "You mentioned earlier that your husband indicated an interest in furthering his career as an airline pilot. Do you know what steps he took to pursue this path, what his plans and ambitions were relative to that?"

Cal interrupted, "You're asking multiple questions."

"Sorry," said Tony. "Let's take them one at a time. Do you know what steps Bobby took to pursue a career as an airline pilot?"

"Well, he was spending a lot of time as a flight instructor. He told me that he needed more piloting time to build up his hours. He also borrowed our neighbor's airplane now and then and made little trips like the one he took when he crashed. He also had lots of friends who were pilots. They wrote letters on his behalf."

"What were their names?"

"I don't really know them. Bobby never brought his friends by."

"Do you think you could try to find some of those letters?"

Annie nodded.

"Is that a yes?" Cal asked.

"Yes." Then Annie said, "He was going to upgrade soon to copilot."

Her lawyer interrupted again, "Annie, just answer the questions."

Annie flushed, "Oh, I'm sorry." She looked down, clearly embarrassed by the reprimand. Tony took advantage of her slip-up. "What makes you believe that Viscount was going to make him a copilot? Did he have anything in writing from the company that said they were going to do that?"

"I don't know if there was anything in writing, but he said they told him he'd be in the next class. That's why he worked so hard to keep flying. He also thought that, with some experience in the pilot seat at Viscount, he could eventually get a job with a major airline—probably in about two years. That was his goal. That was right before his trip to Vicksburg. He was real excited before he left."

"Do you know if he applied at any other companies for a pilot's job before he died?"

Annie bristled when Tony said the word died. He was throwing questions at her fast. She looked over at her lawyer.

Cal interrupted. "I think we need a little break. Does anyone object?"

"That's fine," Tony said. "I could use a fresh cup of coffee myself."

Josey got up and headed for the restroom. A few seconds after she'd locked herself into a stall, Annie walked into the restroom and started sobbing.

Oh shoot, Josey thought. This is awkward. I don't need to be in here with her. Trying to avoid conversation, she left the stall and went to the sink to wash her hands and get out of there fast. But she couldn't avoid Annie, who was clearly distressed. "I'm so sorry, Annie," she said gently. "I know this must be difficult for you. Why don't you just sit over here on this little couch and take some time to clear your head."

Josey could tell that Annie was comfortable with her. She figured there wasn't anyone there who really understood the pain Annie was going through. The lawyers, hers included, seemed so cold. It was just a job to them.

"Thank you, Mrs. Cantwell. I know I probably shouldn't be talking to you, but this is so hard."

Josey gave her an empathetic nod, trying not to encourage conversation.

Annie looked at her wedding ring and began to twist it around on her finger, at the same time moving it up and down without actually taking it off. "Bobby wasn't himself the last few months. I just don't understand it all. He was real distant and wouldn't talk to me much. He was angry all the time. I was really starting to worry about our relationship. Actually, I don't know what he saw in me in the first place. I'm just a quiet, plain country girl. He is—was—so handsome. He was tall, and those blue eyes could melt your heart. Anyway, when he said he was going to be upgraded, I was hoping that things might start to get better. Oh my, I shouldn't have told you that stuff, should I?" She started to cry again.

Josey felt trapped, but she just couldn't leave this poor woman alone right now. She was torn about staying and didn't want to appear self-serving as this information might be helpful, but her natural curiosity won out.

"Do you mind if I smoke?" Annie asked. She pulled out a long, thin brown cigarette with a gold stripe around the filter. She looked at Josey with a plea in her eyes.

Josey nodded in spite of the no smoking sign that hung on the wall of the ladies' room.

"Wow! Those are strong!" Josey exclaimed as the smoke drifted by her nose. Trying to be sensitive to Annie's anguish, she painfully endured the lingering pungent smell of the cigarettes.

"Yeah. Bobby always brought these back from his trips. I sort of got used to them. My one and only really bad habit." Annie drew in deeply and exhaled slowly.

Josey gently put her hand on Annie's shoulder and picked up on her previous comments. "It's okay. I'm sure your relationship problems aren't an issue here. We all go through those stages in our lives. Don't let it worry you."

"Thank you again, Ms. Cantwell. Could we please just keep this between you and me?"

"Of course." Josey was glad that Annie was once again attempting to maintain that professional distance. She didn't like being put on the spot like that.

Josey and Annie walked into the conference room together just as the rest of the group was sitting back down. Josey refreshed her coffee cup and returned to her seat.

Everyone could tell that Annie had been crying. They gave her a chance to get another cup of coffee.

The deposition continued.

"Where were we?" Tony asked.

The court reporter looked at her tape. "Do you know if he applied at any other companies for a pilot's job before he died?"

Annie hesitated. "I'm not sure. I know he subscribed to an online service that posted airline jobs and the qualifications they were looking for."

"Do you know what the qualifications are to be a major airline pilot?" asked Tony.

"No, but he said he met them."

Tony picked up the pace even more. His slow drawl disappeared and his tone became sharp and intimidating. "Did you ever see Bobby's logbooks or any other records of his flying?"

"No."

"Do you know anything else about the qualifications to be a pilot for a major airline?"

"Not really."

"Do you know what Bobby's qualifications were?"

"Well, he told me he had lots of hours. They let him fly in the copilot's seat at Viscount, and his friends told him he had what it takes.

He really liked to fly."

"Did Bobby ever go into any detail about his flight experience with you other than telling you he had lots of hours and his friends said he had what it takes?"

"Well, uh, uh. I guess not."

"Did you ever fly with Bobby?"

"No."

"Do you know if he ever flew in bad weather before?"

"Well, I think so. Uh ... uh ... well, I really can't say. I never thought about it before. He could have."

The deposition went on for another hour, and Annie's testimony didn't reveal anything of value to the defense except that she and her husband didn't seem to communicate much.

Tony and Josey were able to catch a late flight back to Texas, both preferring to sleep in their own beds rather than stay in a hotel, although Josey was somewhat disappointed that she wouldn't get a chance to see the ducks.

Even though Josey hadn't been much more than an observer at the deposition, she was drained. She could only imagine that Tony felt the same. During the entire day, he had seemed totally composed and in control, but she couldn't get rid of that irksome feeling in the pit of her stomach that told her something was not what it seemed.

During the flight, they chatted a little about the case. Hearing Annie's deposition had been valuable to her. She gave Tony a few questions that he hadn't thought of to ask Annie, which he seemed to appreciate. Other than that, they spoke very little until they landed.

Josey didn't mention her brief encounter with Annie.

Chapter 6

Bobby Cisco

Bobby Cisco's mood vacillated from anger to frustration as he returned home after a visit to the human resources department where he had enquired about a pilot's position at Viscount—furious because they'd told him he still needed to gain more experience before they'd put him in a pilot's seat.

"How would they know anyway? They didn't even look at my logbooks!" He slammed his flight bag against the wall. "What a joke! They just don't want me to leave the job I have as flight engineer and mechanic. They're just screwing me around."

Annie came in from the kitchen to greet him. "Are you okay, honey?" Annie asked. "You seem angry."

"Those people wouldn't know a good pilot if an astronaut walked up to them!" Bobby said. "I know I'm a good pilot. You know the pilots at Viscount let me fly sometimes, and they say I'm a good stick. How many people get a chance to take over the controls of a C-130 or a DC-8? If I can fly those, I can fly anything. Plus, I have all that flight instructor time."

"I thought it was against company policy to work on the side," Annie said.

"Shut up. You don't know anything about it. I tell you what it is—they're just dangling the carrot in front of me. They need me where I am—they're getting two jobs out of me for the price of one. I just need a break ... just give me a chance!"

In a huff, he plopped down on the beige, faux-suede sofa, turned on the TV, and tuned in to the end of a news report just as correspondents were attempting to interview Alberto Murillo, a wealthy entrepreneur from San Salvador. Although Bobby had missed the content, he could tell that they were accusing Murillo of crooked dealings. "Hey, I've seen this guy before," Bobby said, trying to recall the event. The man on TV looked familiar. Bobby turned his full attention to the news program. The reporters grimaced as Murillo flicked them off, got into his limo, and drove away.

"Damn, I missed the first part of the report. I wonder what he did."

"What are you mumbling about?" Annie asked

as she sat down next to him. "Something interesting on TV?"

"Nothing important. Just thought I recognized someone. I was wrong," he lied.

Chapter 7

Bobby Cisco

Bobby recalled his last trip to San Salvador in Central America. As he'd sat at the bar in the La Taverna del Sol café near the Zona Rosa, the ritzy and exclusive restaurant and nightlife district, he'd seen a sophisticated man with Royce Allemand. They were seated at a table in the back corner. Bobby realized that the man with Allemand was Alberto Murillo.

Allemand flew to Central America often. As vice president of Viscount Air Transport, he headed the international operations and system planning department. Part of his responsibilities included working with airports and governments with regard to the system negotiating landing rights and facilities.

Bobby always sensed something was shifty about Allemand, so it hadn't surprised him to see them together. He began to wonder about Allemand's relationship with a man like Murillo.

He hadn't had to wait long to satisfy his curiosity. Allemand had flown on Bobby's next trip to San Salvador.

Personally, Bobby thought Allemand was aloof and even quite condescending—characteristics demonstrated on the trip when a new-hire flight attendant came into the cockpit crying. "Can't you do something?" she begged. "He embarrassed me in front of all the passengers." She wiped the mascara from her cheeks with a tissue.

"Who?" the captain asked.

"That Allemand guy," she replied. "What makes him so special?"

"What did you do?" the captain enquired.

"I didn't recognize him. Sure, I knew his name and position, but I've never seen him or a picture of him. How was I supposed to know he was our VP? He didn't need to get so bent out of shape. Do you think he can get me fired?"

"Forget it. It happens all the time. He complains so much now that our bosses seem to let it ride or we wouldn't have any employees left. I guess the big shots think he does his job okay so they ignore his insensitivity to the employees. You'll be okay. Like I said, forget it."

Bobby heard the complaint, but ignored it—his mind a world away, reflecting on the newscast he'd recently seen. He couldn't stop thinking about the connection between Allemand and Murillo.

The flight arrived at Monseñor Óscar Arnulfo Romero International Airport, formerly known as Comalapa International Airport, at around ten thirty in the morning. After a brief trek through customs, the crew and other employees, including Allemand, were shuttled to a downtown hotel. The crew sat in silence during the forty-five minute trek to town, their spirits dampened by Allemand's rude outburst on the plane.

They arrived at the hotel just before lunch anxious to get to their air-conditioned rooms; the heat and humidity were already stifling.

"Hey, Bobby. Want to go get lunch with us?" the first officer asked after waiting for Allemand to disappear.

"Not now," Bobby replied. "I just want to rest for a while. Maybe tonight. We'll go party in the Zona Rosa."

The captain checked in for the whole crew and gave them all their keys. Bobby rushed to his room and donned his civilian clothes, putting on a hat that covered his unruly thatch of blond hair. He planned to follow Allemand and didn't want to stand out in a country where the majority of the people had dark hair. A pair of dark sunglasses completed his attempt at a disguise.

He took the elevator down to the lobby and waited in a corner, out of sight, until he spotted Allemand leaving.

Allemand took off on foot, and Bobby lurked behind, staying a safe distance to avoid detection.

It was a typical day in the city; traffic was backed up for about ten blocks while workmen scurried about fixing the abundant potholes in the road.

San Salvador, Central America's most populated city, bustled with activity. The pollution, noise, chaos, and crowds could be overwhelming at times. This turned out to be an advantage for Bobby as he followed Allemand with stealth and caution.

Allemand and Murillo met again at the Taverna del Sol where Bobby had first spotted the pair. They greeted each other with a brisk handshake and settled into a booth toward the back of the café in a dim area near the door to the kitchen. The booths had high backs and provided a false sense of privacy. The smell of spicy beef searing in the kitchen blended with the acrid smell of cigars and cigarettes that drifted through the cafe.

The two men lit their own cigarettes, and Murillo summoned a waiter with a crisp snap of his fingers. The waiter, who had spotted the men entering the room, already stood at attention, awaiting his summons. In his attempt to please, his haste caused him to trip as he headed to the booth. He managed to make a fortunate, but awkward, recovery.

As Bobby observed the scene, he surmised that one or both of the two men were special customers at this restaurant.

The lunch crowd in these Latin American countries could spend two to three hours enjoying their midday repast. The crowd flocked to the outside tables first and worked their way to the back of the restaurant. As luck would have it, Bobby grabbed a booth within earshot of the two men. He sat with his back turned away from them. The couple spoke up so they could hear each other as the noise level continued to escalate—obviously not realizing their voices were carrying so far.

Bobby, keeping his voice low, ordered a beer and a salad. He concentrated on the conversation in the next booth.

"We need six next week," Murillo said.

"Not a problem. Just make sure you have the right documents. The last shipment had a glitch. We almost had to send one back," Allemand replied.

"We have more requests than we can fill. I'm thinking of expanding." Murillo paused. Bobby heard him take a deep drag of the slender cigarette. "Maybe in another city."

Bobby heard bits and pieces of the confusing conversation, but grasped enough to capture the nature of their business. He thought he'd heard it all. You could see stuff like this on TV or at the movies, but here were two men in a restaurant in San Salvador discussing a conspiracy so appalling even he was stunned.

Should I call the authorities? How could I prove anything? Would anyone believe me without evidence? Doubtful. He started thinking about his flights and tried to remember anything unusual.

His revulsion didn't last long. He wondered how he could use this information to his advantage. He started formulating his plan. No. He wouldn't go to the authorities—not yet. He decided to follow Allemand during the next few trips and gather concrete evidence. He'd blackmail Allemand and put pressure on him to get the flight department to promote him to copilot and perhaps make some extra cash on the side.

Characteristic of Bobby, lacking any semblance of conscience, he thought with smug satisfaction, At last, I'm going to get what I want.

He paid the bill in cash and got up, careful not to show his face to the table behind him. He left the restaurant and hurried back to the hotel hoping no one would see him.

—✦—

Bobby had three more trips from Dallas/Fort Worth to San Salvador that month. Things were moving according to his plan until one afternoon his constant daydreaming caught him off guard, and he got sloppy.

As Allemand exited the café to return to the hotel, he spotted Bobby loitering outside smoking a cigarette.

Allemand started the conversation in his elitist tone, "Hello, Bobby. What a coincidence bumping into you here. Lousy weather, eh?"

Bobby thanked the gods for the hot weather—covering the fact that his sweat came from fear rather than the insipid heat. He hoped

Allemand didn't get suspicious. "Yeah, well, I've seen most of this city, but I like this area. It's pretty and seems a little safer than most. I walk a lot. Gotta keep in shape. There isn't much else to do in this town." Bobby found himself rambling.

"Hmm. I see your point," Allemand said, his voice haughty. "I heard about this restaurant from one of the crew members. Thought I'd check it out."

Yeah, right, thought Bobby. He decided at that moment that the time had come to get that promotion.

Bobby sensed that Allemand had suspicions about this encounter. He noticed Allemand's brow lifting slightly as his eyes squinted, giving the impression that he didn't believe in coincidences.

—◆—

Allemand had good reason to be uneasy. A couple of hours after he arrived home, he received the call from Bobby. "I know what you're doing, and I have it documented. I've put my proof in a safe place, so don't screw around with me. I want a quarter of a million, and I want to fly. Get me the money and get me upgraded. Now!"

Chapter 8

The sight mesmerized Royce Allemand as he stood outside the door of Alberto Murillo's San Salvador mansion. More like a fortress, he thought. This was the first time he had been to Murillo's home; they usually met at the Taverna, one of Murillo's many holdings. Since being spotted by Cisco, they had decided to meet in a more private place.

"Get yourself together," Allemand said aloud as he knocked on the massive door. He dreaded the meeting, knowing Murillo would be furious.

Humberto, Murillo's native servant, answered the door, which opened up to a large foyer with glistening marble floors. The walls on each side were covered with portraits of aristocratic men and women from different eras, spanning what seemed to be decades.

The fifty-four-year-old Allemand stretched his five-foot-three frame trying to look taller. He took slow strides to draw attention away from his distinctive limp caused by a bout of polio contracted at the age of ten. It had left him with an underdeveloped right leg that was shorter than his left. The expensive special shoes he bought to balance his gate did little to disguise it.

After ten years at Viscount, Allemand had managed to climb the ladder to the second-highest position in the company. He had a strong presence in the aviation industry, and his ultimate goal was to start his own airline. To do that, he needed capital. That's where Murillo came in.

Humberto led Allemand to the right and down a long hallway until they reached the library that also served as Murillo's office. Row after row of leather-bound books in Spanish and English lined the walls. The heavy brocade curtains were closed to keep out the heat. Although the room was cool, the darkness was oppressive and claustrophobic in spite of the expansive area.

Murillo, dressed in an open-necked polo shirt and fine tailored slacks, was seated in a large high-backed chair sipping a brandy and smoking a cigar, the potent scent wafting throughout the room.

— ✦ —

As Allemand approached, Murillo eyed him warily. He didn't think much of Royce

Allemand—an insecure social climber obsessed with his looks. His ebony-black, slicked-back hair looked as if it had been painted on his head. His teeth, yellowed from excessive smoking, ruined any potential appearance of sophistication.

"Royce, please, have a seat. Cigar? It's Cuban. Or brandy?" Murillo asked and looked over at Humberto.

Murillo, tall and aristocratic, looked at home in the elegant surroundings. He came from a wealthy Spanish heritage and a long line of philanthropists and businessmen. His blue-blood veins were lined with steel. Nothing could penetrate them, and nothing could stand in the way of his endeavors.

Allemand pointed to the brandy and sat in a chair facing Murillo. He pulled out his own cigarette with a gold band around the filter and lit it.

Humberto poured brandy into a crystal snifter, handed it graciously to Allemand, and left the room.

Allemand swirled the brandy around in the glass, warming the deep honey-colored liquid in the palm of his hand. He took a sip and looked up at Murillo. "Listen, Alberto, this is serious," Allemand said as a red flush ran up his neck, ending at his cheeks. "He says he has evidence and will expose us."

"So what does he want?" Murillo asked.

"He wants two hundred fifty thousand US dollars and says he wants to be a pilot but—"

"So, negotiate. Give him a couple thousand and make him a pilot," Murillo interrupted in impeccable English.

"You don't understand," Allemand replied. "He said he has insurance in case something happens to him. He won't stop there. I know this is just the tip of the iceberg. He'll keep wanting more. We can't take any chances. We need to be cautious and keep an eye on him. This guy is a cunning opportunist."

"We'll take care of him when the time comes," Murillo said.

"He's been on a number of my flights. From the cockpit gossip I hear, he's a real jerk. Runs around on his wife, loves to gamble, and is really strapped for cash. Guys like that can only cause problems," Allemand blurted.

"Didn't you hear me?" A vein in Murillo's neck bulged and he leaned forward. "I'll take care of it. Don't worry about it. My people will keep an eye on him. We'll make sure he doesn't get in the way." His voice was even and crisp. "Of course, there are ways to resolve the issue permanently," Murillo continued as he twisted a large gold ring back and forth on his finger. The ring was an heirloom with the family crest engraved in the gold and a large diamond mounted in the intricate craftsmanship. It had been in the family for several generations and had passed down to him from his father.

"I believe permanent to you means something more permanent than it does to me. Let's wait." Allemand took a large sip of the brandy.

"When the time is right, it will be handled." Murillo took a puff of the cigar and watched as the smoke drifted up, an eerie cloud in the grayness of the room.

"Just make sure. Prison is not what I envision as a retirement village." Allemand stared into his glass.

"We have other business to discuss. Get a grip on yourself," Murillo ordered.

Murillo casually sipped his own brandy as he and Allemand discussed the status of their next transaction.

"Alberto, I think it's time for me to retire from this," Allemand finally said. "I just can't handle the stress anymore. This Cisco problem just accentuates it. You can run this operation without me. I can't stand the pressure of watching over my shoulder day and night."

Although Murillo was sick and tired of Allemand's constant whining, he couldn't afford to lose him yet. "You don't understand, Royce, my friend. There's only one option in this partnership, and it is not retirement. Need I say more?" Murillo ended the conversation with a smooth, yet sinister tone.

Allemand swallowed hard and just shook his head.

Chapter 9

A few days later, Murillo's man followed Bobby to Vicksburg, Mississippi, where he found him kicking up his heels drinking, gambling, and cavorting.

Murillo called Allemand before sunrise. "It is time to initiate the plan."

"Why do I have to do this?" Allemand protested from his office in Dallas, fearful and with good reason. "What if I get caught?"

"Just do as I say, and everything will work out," Murillo instructed him.

"You want me to be the patsy, don't you? Can't we try something else?

"Look, don't waste any more precious moments. The clock is ticking," Murillo interrupted. "Just get it done."

Allemand checked the weather. The front moving across the south would work in their favor.

As usual, Allemand arrived at 5:30 in the

morning, well before most of the Viscount employees. The company worked with a skeleton crew until eight in the morning.

He called the only crew scheduler on duty. "Vick, you aren't busy now, are you?"

"No," Vick replied. "It's quiet. Nothing going on."

"I need to talk to you about some scheduling problems we're having in Central America. Can you break away and come up to my office for a minute?"

"How long do you think it'll take?"

"Maybe ten, fifteen minutes, max."

"No problem. If it's more than ten minutes, I have to change the voice mail message. It'll only take a second and I'll be right there," Vick said.

Royce Allemand, limping as usual, left his office and hustled awkwardly toward the staircase. He hobbled down to the first floor. Allemand slipped through the door to the stairwell that was adjacent to Vick's office and waited until he heard the door shut as Vick left his office. Then he opened the door to the hallway, and peered out. He watched the elevator door shut after Vick stepped in.

The halls were empty and the lights were dim. Allemand went to Vick's cubicle, grabbed the scheduler's phone, and dialed Bobby's cell phone number. "Bobby," he said, disguising his voice. "We need you back to work. The flight engineer on the two o'clock flight called in sick, and we don't have anyone else available."

"Hey, this is my day off. You can't make me come in." Bobby's voice reflected his anger.

"Sorry, dude. Just doing my job. Complain to someone else. But I suggest you get here."

"Where's the supervisor? Let me talk to him," Cisco barked.

"No one here but me. I just got the call, and I'll be in trouble if I don't have a replacement before the boss gets in."

"Yeah, yeah, okay. I'm coming, but someone is gonna hear about this!"

"Like I said, just doing my job," Allemand said. He hunched over the phone trying to camouflage his presence, even though no one was in the office. He smiled with sardonic pleasure and thought, Cisco won't want to miss that trip. He thinks he's getting ready to go to upgrade school, so he won't rock the boat now.

Allemand's fear subsided after he talked to Bobby. This could work. No matter what happens now, he thought, Cisco won't be a problem to anyone anymore.

Allemand hurried back up the stairwell to his office to find Vick standing inside the doorway. "Sorry, Vick. I had to run to the rest room. Sit down. Let's go over those schedules now."

Chapter 10

Bobby Cisco

Even at five o'clock in the morning, the intermittent ringing from the slot machines permeated the room as Bobby Cisco punched the "end" button on his cell phone. He'd walked out into the hallway to get better reception.

"That S-O-B! I knew that bastard would find a way to get rid of me!" His animosity rose as he made his way back to the bar where Val, his "other woman," unknown to Bobby's wife, Annie, waited. "Well, that's okay. They will pay for this in a big way," Bobby said, the hatred in his voice cutting the air.

He hadn't recognized the voice of the scheduler on the other end of the line. Must be new, Bobby thought. The new guys always got the lousy schedules. His company had a hard time keeping people. Once they got a little experience, they departed as fast as the company could cut the last paycheck so they could work at an airline with better benefits. He would too—soon.

Bobby took one last puff of his expensive cigar and gulped the last of his drink. He set the glass down on the elegant black marble bar and stood, throwing a five-dollar tip at the bartender.

He grabbed Val and pulled her from the next stool. The petite, busty blonde, sporting a tight and provocative lime-green jumpsuit, winced as Bobby's vise-like grip almost bruised her arm.

"Let's go. I gotta get back to work."

"Are you sure you should be flying now?" Val said. "You've been up all night, and you've had a lot to drink."

"Look, don't get on my case. Just get your stuff and let's get out of here."

"Bobby, is everything all right? What happened? You should be celebrating; you just won five thousand dollars at the poker table."

"I said ... look, just let it go. I don't need another wife nagging on me!" Bobby said with open disgust. "Just get me to the airport."

"Okay, Bobby. I'm sorry. Loosen up on my arm, please." Val tugged at Bobby's hand.

Val always picked Bobby up when he came into town, and she dropped everything to be with him during his stay. They had met in the casino on his first trip to Vicksburg and made it a point to meet whenever he came to town. Born and raised there in Mississippi, she worked as a receptionist at a local accounting firm. Bobby played her just like the others, making her think he would leave his wife for her.

The truth be known, Bobby didn't intend to leave his wife—at least not for a cheap floozy like Val. She was a good time to him, nothing more.

They always stayed at the same hotel. It had about a hundred rooms and was attached to a quaint gambling casino floating next to the banks of the Mississippi River. Small gambling meccas like this were the rage and were making their way up and down the Mississippi, reminiscent of the old riverboat gambler days.

Bobby moved with a swagger that suggested a condescending attitude. It came through loud and clear to men and women alike, but he had just enough boyish charm that they overlooked it.

He never left home without his leather bomber jacket, which he wore as though it was a symbol of his prowess. He always had a story to tell about his flying escapades, none of them true.

He gambled in Vicksburg because the people there treated him like a king. For the moment it served him well, much better than being in a big city like Vegas or Atlantic City. Bobby was a regular, and everyone knew him. That made him feel important, and he liked that.

Bobby's mind drifted off to a luxury suite on a private island. My own jet. Maybe a yacht. Yeah, definitely a yacht. He could almost smell the caramel tones and peppery sweetness of his favorite expensive cigar as he lounged with a bevy of beauties on the edge of a crystal-blue ocean.

Val tripped over the stool and bumped Bobby forward, jolting him from his daydream. "Watch it! Klutz! Let's get out of here," he said.

The sun barely appeared through the cloud cover as it peeked above the horizon. Thunderstorms were typical as the end of May approached. A fine mist moistened Bobby's face. The air was muggy and heavy, but calm and still, the way it feels just before a storm.

A little rain and a few clouds wouldn't stand in Bobby's way. He loved to push the limits and treated life like a game. He'd had some close calls, but always made it through at the end.

"Lucky I took the plane this time," he mumbled to himself, staggering a little from the effects of the alcohol.

Bobby called his friend Steve at the airport. Steve always helped him fuel up and get ready for his flight. Someone else answered. "Steve isn't here. Name's Claude. I'm filling in for him."

"No matter. You'll do. Time for me to go. Run over to the airport and get the plane ready. Gotta get back."

Bobby hopped into Val's 1971 Karmann Ghia convertible for the seven-mile drive back to the Vicksburg Municipal Airport where he had parked his airplane.

Val lamented about his departure, but that only increased Bobby's irritability. Tired of her constant clinging to him and whining, he made the decision to cut the relationship off. In his typical style, he'd just disappear from her life. She'd get over it.

Without so much as a backward glance or good-bye, Bobby jumped out of the car and headed toward the airplane.

"Bye, Bobby. Thanks for a good time. Bastard," Val muttered as she drove off in a huff.

Claude was fueling the airplane when Bobby arrived. That saved some time. Bobby did a cursory preflight and walked around the airplane, paying little attention to the task. His mind wasn't focused on the flight but on his annoyance at having to get back to Texas. He took the rules with a grain of salt. He jumped into the Cessna 172, a single-engine prop that he'd borrowed from his friend for the trip back to Texas. Still waiting for Claude, he pulled his logbook out of his kit bag and jotted down the flight and time notations to document his trip from Arlington. He tossed the book on the seat next to him and shouted to Claude as he pulled the hose out of the airplane, "Let's roll!"

Bobby glanced at the clouds once again. He knew the weather was deteriorating, but he never let the elements get in his way.

Bobby looked around as he taxied. He passed the small red brick terminal building that looked like an old home dating back many years that someone had converted to offices. Nearby were a couple of hangars. A lone sign stuck out of the ground: Learn to Fly Here. One small twin-engine and a couple of single-engine propeller airplanes were parked on the tarmac. A small fire station stood due south of the terminal building.

Vicksburg was an uncontrolled airport, and Bobby didn't need anyone to clear him for takeoff. He blew off the last minute checks. In a couple of minutes he was in the air, making a quick turn to the west and heading home.

He crossed over the Mississippi River climbing at a rate of about 700 feet per minute. When he hit 850 feet, he experienced a slight engine stutter, just enough to catch his attention but not startle him. He glanced around the cockpit, pausing as he looked in the back.

He ran through the checklist, speaking aloud, trying to remain calm, "Fuel selector on." He looked almost straight down from his right shoulder.

Bobby was trained for emergencies. The alcohol was still affecting him. He had to stay calm.

"Carb heat on." It was a muggy day; you never know.

"Okay, calm yourself, Bobby. Mixture full rich. Magnetos to both." He glanced to the left side of the yoke just above his left knee. He noticed his knee was starting to vibrate. My nerves!

"Damn, I need a landmark. Where's that chart?" Bobby stretched his arm and torso full length as he reached to grab the chart from the floor of the aircraft.

The cloud cover was expanding. Bobby's visibility was diminishing as he crossed into Louisiana. Popping in and out of the clouds, he decided to climb to receive better radio signals from the Monroe navigation aids. It was becoming difficult to maintain visual flight rules without calling for a flight plan.

Bobby grabbed the map and lifted his head. His throat tightened, his neck grew stiff. He knew the moment was coming.

The airplane was careening toward the trees.

—◆—

A lone man working outside on his farm heard what sounded like an explosion and saw a flash. The aircraft crashed just over the Mississippi/Louisiana state line near the town of Fortune Ford, Louisiana, a fitting epitaph for a guy like Bobby Cisco, whose fortune-hunting days were now laid to rest.

—◆—

When the FAA and the NTSB got to the crash site, the charred wreckage littered the area.

The loose contents of the airplane, along with many of Bobby's personal belongings, had been thrown free from the craft on impact. There was a small fire, which had led to the explosion. The body, charred beyond recognition, lay mangled in the wreckage.

Now came the task of sorting through things to try to determine the cause of the crash—and Bobby's death. The search team started the tedious job of collecting the remains and putting the pieces of the puzzle together.

Chapter 11

Josey jumped into Brad's car for their visit to the Benton Air Hangar where the ill-fated aircraft had last been serviced.

"How was your trip? Are you going to keep the case?" he asked her.

"Honestly, even though Tony McIntyre was above board, he was condescending and almost mean to Annie. But the case really intrigues me, so I'm going to go ahead with it—at least for now." As Brad negotiated the traffic, she continued, "Brad, we haven't had a chance to talk since I left for Memphis. What's the deal with Natasha? How did you meet her? Is she one of your old covert spook friends? She is definitely spooky—just pops up out of nowhere. But, holy-moly, can she cook!"

Brad winked. "The less you know, the better. Let me say this, though—if she likes you, you are gold. If she doesn't ... beware. I can't tell you about the last guy who crossed her. She may be old, but she can definitely hold her own."

"Great. She'll probably sick that scary little monster on me."

"Monster?"

"The dog."

"That's new—she used to have a scary black cat."

—✦—

Josey's heels echoed as she and Brad walked into the hangar owned by Benton Air. The security guard let them in and escorted them a short way into the cavernous structure. The only aircraft inside was undergoing a basic maintenance check.

"Wow, this place is impeccably clean," Josey said. She guessed that special pains had been taken to tidy up after the accident.

The guard pointed to a door on the right side of the hangar about midway down. "There's the office you want. This is as far as I go—I have to get back to my post," he said.

Along the way, Josey recounted her concern about the Cisco case. "Brad, that poor Annie Cisco. From what little she said about her relationship with her husband, I'm surprised they were still together. She didn't know anything about his work or how he planned to get an airline job. I don't think they talked much. From the scuttlebutt I got from Tony, I think her husband cheated on her right and left. What a creep! They definitely had a communication problem." She slowed her pace a bit, then stopped, and turned to Brad. "I got cornered with her in the ladies' room. She was so upset, I felt she needed a little empathy. I have a feeling that she really wanted to confide in me about something but was fearful about letting it out. I think she's holding back something important and possibly incriminating." Josey shook her head.

"Well, if she did, you'll find it," Brad responded. "I don't know anyone who is better at digging out the truth than you. The only time I actually surprised you was when I gave you the necklace. Your expression was priceless."

Brad tugged at Josey's arm. "Let's keep moving."

Josey picked up the pace. "I'm starting to regret that I took on this case, Brad. I really don't have the time anymore, and like I said, I'm not sure I like that lawyer—I feel he's trying to manipulate me. He really tore into Annie. She could barely maintain her composure. Seems to me he would have gained more from her if he'd appeared a little more empathetic."

"I don't know—kind of sounds like a fascinating one to me," Brad said. "Viscount is a strange company. You might learn some interesting stuff. If you need me to do a little nosing around, just let me know. In the meantime, be careful."

"Don't worry—you're number one on my speed dial." They had almost reached the office. "Well, I was surprised to hear about another accident," she said. "That makes three in a row! These unsolved crashes are starting to generate fear and rumors. I was a nervous flyer before, but now I'm almost afraid to get on any airplane." Even the thought sent shivers through her body.

"This third accident at Benton Air seems like a no-brainer. The way I see it, the captain has a heart attack, the copilot can't take the stress and loses it—airplane crashes. Case closed," Brad commented.

"What do you think we're going to learn here in this hangar?" Josey asked.

"I don't know, but we just need to cover all our bases."

Josey and Brad had stayed within a lined walkway around the edge of the cavernous building until they reached the office. They were there to meet with the maintenance chief, the last person to sign off on the airplane.

"This facility is not all that impeccable," Brad said as he spotted a pack of cigarettes on the floor wedged behind a wastebasket, barely noticeable. He leaned over to pick it up. "Someone must have dropped these. The cost of cigarettes these days is outrageous. Don't know why anyone continues to smoke. I'll give them to the chief." He stuck the pack in his pocket.

"Wait, let me see those cigarettes." Josey held out her hand. "Is that Spanish on the label?"

"Here," he said as he pulled them back out and handed the pack to her. "What is it?" Brad asked, staring at her as she took them from him.

Josey looked at the pack and pulled a cigarette out. She sniffed it. "Nothing really. I think these are the same cigarettes that Annie Cisco was smoking at the deposition. Guess these are more popular than I thought. Maybe they're cheaper than American cigarettes so airline employees smuggle them into the States to save money. When you have the habit, maybe you'll smoke anything, especially when you can save money."

Josey rolled the cigarette around in her fingers, quietly reflecting on her conversation with Annie, and then stuck it back in the pack. "Here," she handed the pack back to Brad, who took one last look and put them into his coat pocket.

Together they surveyed the hangar as they stood outside the office waiting for the chief of maintenance to arrive.

"I don't see any relationship among the accidents," Josey said. "With three in a row like this, you'd be inclined to think there might be some common link. But the accidents happened to different airlines. It has to be coincidence."

"Okay, we know that the copilot on each flight was a rookie. That's the only common denominator I can find so far," Brad said.

"Now that I think about it, the weather in every accident was nasty, and the engines inexplicably lost power before each crash, and they all crashed into water," Josey said. "But the captain had a heart attack on the Benton Air flight."

"Well, was the heart attack caused by the problem or was it the problem?" Brad asked. "We don't know for sure, do we?"

"The CVR tapes don't reveal anything useful," Josey said, referring to the cockpit voice recorder that was standard on all US multi-engine turbine powered aircraft carrying six or more passengers if two pilots are required.

"Only a really strung out crew. Seems they really lost it at the end. What a way to go," Brad added.

"Let's try to stay focused on our mission here for now. We'll see what we can find out," Josey said.

"Right-o. Here comes Carlos. Let's get on with it." Brad waved to Carlos Pena, chief of maintenance at Benton Air for ten years, as he walked their way from the other side of the hangar. Carlos ushered them into his small office.

"I'm afraid you're wasting your time here," said Carlos, his voice emphasizing he did not welcome the interruption from his busy schedule. Josey surmised that, after being constantly interrogated about the accident, Carlos might be defensive and irritable. He was a short, stocky, dark-skinned Latino, and the buttons of his Benton Air overalls were bulging. Josey couldn't think of the name of the fragrance he was wearing, but knew she would be smelling it for hours. Carlos shook hands with Josey and Brad.

"Well, let's just take a quick look at the records," Brad said. "Can't go back without doing my job."

"Here," Carlos said as he handed Brad the logs. "We have gone over everything here with a fine-toothed comb and still can't come up with a maintenance reason for the incident, but the NTSB and our team are still trying to put the pieces together. The techs on duty didn't have contact with the pilots before the flight and don't recall anything unusual."

Brad noticed that the last record in the maintenance log for that airplane had been signed off by a Chuck Finley with A&P Contracting Services, a contract maintenance company.

"Do you use contract help much?" Brad asked.

"It's cheaper for us to field out some of this work. We just started using A&P," Carlos said.

"Nothing out of the ordinary here," Brad said as he closed the book.

Back in the hangar, Josey and Brad chatted a little more with the chief and some of the maintenance technicians, and like Carlos, they were unable to drum up any new thoughts or ideas.

"Thanks, Carlos—that's it," said Brad. "Let's go, Josey."

Josey and Brad left, frustrated about the lack of support. They walked in silence to the parking lot.

As they stood by Brad's car preparing to leave, Brad turned to her and said, "I just remembered. That company—A&P Contracting Services—was the same group that worked on the airplane that crashed in New Orleans. I knew it rang a bell. I think I saw something about them in a news clip not long ago—and it wasn't good. I think I'll do a little checking on them." Perplexed, he brushed his fingers through his hair.

Josey nodded. Brad's instincts were usually right on.

Chapter 12

Josey arrived back home from the meeting at the Benton Air hangar mid-afternoon to find Rene in the kitchen eating from a large bowl. Her hair was tied into a loose ponytail, several strands falling around her face. "Hey, Mom. Want something to eat? This quinoa salad you made is amazing."

"What quinoa salad? Let me see." Josey grabbed a spoon out of the drawer, took the bowl out of Rene's hand, and scooped out a large bite. "Oh, my God. Is there any left?"

"So if you didn't make it ... Natasha?"

"Of course." They turned around to see Natasha standing just inside the door from the garage. She had lost the beret to reveal silver hair pulled back in a tight bun at the nape of her neck. Boris stood at attention next to her. Luc ran over to Josey and clung to her side.

"If you continue to cook like this, we will never let you go. Thanks, Natasha," said Josey.

"I need milk." She grabbed the milk and, with Boris at her side, took off.

"Did you ask Brad about Natasha?" Rene asked after the door leading to the garage apartment clicked shut.

"Yes, but he was really vague. Maybe we'll learn more later. She is a strange duck." But I don't care what she did or where she came from if she keeps cooking like that. I absolutely must get to work on the Viscount case." Josey waved at Rene and headed to her office.

Back at her desk, she shoved nonessential papers aside, pulled out the documents relating to the Viscount case, and began flipping through the exhibits. Viscount had sent her a stack of papers that measured almost twelve inches. Included were copies of Cisco's logbooks retrieved by the FAA investigators at the crash site in Fortune Ford, a resume that appeared to have been prepared within the last couple of months of his accident, some past income tax returns provided by Annie Cisco, a variety of military commendations, copies of licenses and other flight documents, four separate depositions, and pay stubs from Viscount Air Transport and the flight schools where he had taught.

Cisco had kept two logbooks that tracked every airplane and all the hours he had flown. The logbook was a pilot's sacred journal. A pilot would rather lose the family jewels than lose his logbooks. Both of Cisco's books were standard issue—the first, a small book in which he had recorded his first year of private flying during his tour in the navy. Pretty typical. He had soloed sooner than most, got his private pilot's certificate after about forty-five hours in a single-engine aircraft, and moved on to receive the commercial certificate, with single-engine, multi-engine, and instrument ratings, just after he hit the 250-hour mark.

Bobby had abandoned the small book and started documenting his flight hours in a different and larger logbook after he reached 400 hours, about the same time he got his flight instructor's certificate and started teaching ground school and flight training.

After reviewing several pages of the logbooks, Josey noticed that Bobby had a flair for documenting more than just the standard appropriate information one typically saw in a logbook. She raised her eyebrow and sat up, turning her head to the door. "This is incredible. It's more like a diary than a logbook. This guy was nuts!" she called out to Rene. Josey's daughter walked into the office holding another bowl of quinoa, and looked over her shoulder. "Getta load of this, Rene." Josey noticed the bowl of salad. "Glutton," she said.

"Can't help it. This is to die for."

"Cisco recorded all the stuff he did when he was out flying. When his wife gets wind of this, she's going to flip! Look at this ..." Josey lifted the book pointing to the page.

"11/26 ... Aircraft Type-C172 ... Aircraft-N5437S ... GKY-VKS-GKY ... Remarks—a little mischief—Val—what a catch—jackpot ... flying high"

"What airports are GKY and VKS?" asked Rene.

"Arlington, Texas, and Vicksburg, Mississippi. That's where he flew from on his last trip."

"Oh, okay. Go on. Sorry, Mom. I didn't mean to interrupt. I thought I knew most of those codes—can't believe I didn't know the one for my own hometown!" Rene smacked the top of her head, knocking a few more strands of hair over one eye.

"That's understandable," Josey replied, not looking up at Rene. "It used to be F54 until they changed it." She looked back at the printout. "Let's see ... 12/15 ... Cessna 172 Aircraft ID

... yada yada ... GKY-SAT-San Antonio-GKY ... Remarks—some fun ... buzzed the farm, scud running ..."

"Okay, now I feel really dumb," said Rene. "What's scud running?"

Josey explained, "It's hard to define, but basically flying low below a low cloud layer. It's a major cause of general aviation accidents. I count it akin to drunk driving. I worked on another case once in which the pilot also documented scud running along with buzzing in his logbooks. He died too. " She flipped a few more pages of the logbook. "It goes on and on like that. If an airline saw this stuff at an interview, Cisco would be out the door before he could scud run home."

While Rene turned to some paperwork of her own, Josey worked through the document, spot-checking the tail numbers, also called N numbers, of all the aircraft that appeared to look out of place considering his experience. The N marking identifies the aircraft as being registered in the US. She compared the numbers to a list on a website that provided information on just about any aircraft in the United States. She could look up who owned the plane, the type of aircraft—like Piper or Beechcraft—and where the owner kept the plane. The site also provided information on the nature of the flying—like flight instructing, charter or passenger transport.

She loved how technology saved her time. She simply turned on the computer and input a few key words and voila! Answers!

Josey imagined Bobby would be capable flying a single engine airplane and logging the hours in the multi-engine column thinking that nobody would look at the records that closely. During her career, Josey's persistence and attention to detail had paid off over and over, stirring up fear in the minds of those who opposed her in court.

In spite of the unsuitable commentaries noted during his personal flying sprees, Bobby seemed to record his flight instructing time okay.

Josey began to review the section that documented Bobby's flights at Viscount.

"What's this? I thought Cisco was a flight engineer," Josey said out loud. "He's logging his flight engineer time as copilot time. What a cheat!"

"What do you mean, Mom?" Rene placed her partially eaten salad on the side table and put her hands on Josey's shoulders.

"Bobby never flew as a copilot at Viscount. Tony told me he harassed the human resource and flight department about upgrading him so much they tried to avoid him. They claimed they had no intention of upgrading him. I know some pilots who put the flight engineer time in the logbooks and make a separate column or even cross out 'second in command' and put in F/E—for flight engineer—but to document the time like this!" She huffed. "This is falsification of professional documents. I can't believe he thought he could get away with this. Unbelievable."

While this wasn't the first time Josey had seen something like that, it still astounded her that anyone would attempt to falsify flying records. Shaking her head she continued. "What more?" Josey kept reading—enthralled by the fabrications and fascinating annotations.

Just when she thought she had seen it all, a series of notes sparked her curiosity. They gave her an uneasy feeling, one she couldn't quite get a handle on.

"Hey, enough work!" Brad startled Josey and Rene as he sauntered into her office. He had his own key to the house and often welcomed himself into her home unannounced.

"Oh, my gosh! I got so wrapped up in this

stuff that I lost track of time." Josey turned and smiled at Brad and then glanced at her watch.

"Well, we have dinner reservations, so get going," Brad chided her with his half smile.

"Hey, Brad. Try this." Rene shoved the bowl of quinoa at Brad. "Natasha made it. It is amazing."

"Of course." Brad smiled mimicking Natasha. "Someday I'll tell you about her cooking skills, among others."

"Just give me a second," said Josey. "I want to call Tony McIntyre and give him a quick update. Then we can go. Brad, you won't believe this guy, Bobby Cisco. What a trip! Trip. Hey! Get it? Pilot—trip."

"Good one, Mom," Rene first rolled her eyes and then stared at Josey with that typical look implying her mother needed serious help.

"Well, I guess you had to be there," Josey said, still smiling at her clever little remark.

Brad gave Josey the same exaggerated mocking look. "Tell me at dinner. Hurry up now. Is it possible for you to get anywhere on time?"

"Come on," Josey said. "One of my pleasures in life is to have you and everyone else badgering me all the time." She picked up the phone and dialed Tony. As she waited for him to answer, she said, "This Viscount attorney is going to get more ammunition than he bargained for in this case. Just from what I've reviewed so far, I can see some big problems for the Cisco estate."

Chapter 13

Tony McIntyre furrowed his brow as he hung up the phone.

"What is it?" asked Royce Allemand as he walked into Tony's office for a meeting.

"That was Josey Cantwell. You remember, she agreed to assist us as an expert witness in the Cisco case?" Tony looked down at his desk and picked up Josey's book. "Look, I just got this. Here she is." He pointed to Josey's picture on the back of her book. "She sent this with her resume—it's about how to develop a career as a pilot."

Allemand took the book from him, studied her picture, and put it back on the desk. "I guess we're lucky to have her on our side."

"Anyway," Tony continued, "she said she was reviewing the documents we provided when she noticed some major inconsistencies. Bobby also made some strange notations in his logbooks. She didn't have time to discuss them just then, but said she'd get back to me. She thinks he may have falsified some information, and what she's discovered might be helpful to our case."

"Really?" Allemand tapped his pen on the desk. "Did she give you any other details?" He tried to hide his uneasiness by slouching a little in the seat, his legs stretched out with abandon.

"No, just what I said. She's leaving tomorrow morning on a business trip, but said she'd get back to me when she returns. Do you have a particular interest in this?"

"No, not really. Just curious I guess. He worked on several of my trips. Seemed to be a cocky kid." Allemand continued to tap his pen.

"So I've heard. I'm sorry about his untimely demise, but I didn't see many folks here too upset over it." Tony stared at Allemand and looked at the bouncing pen. "We still have some loose ends with Mrs. Cisco's lawsuit," he said. "We don't know why his wife thinks that Bobby was about to be upgraded. And we can't figure out who called him back to work. Right now we have two people—his wife and an apparent girlfriend—who claim someone called. Nobody at the company will come forward and admit it. Even though we announced that no one will be burned for this, we still can't get anyone to fess up. Has anyone talked to you about it, Royce? You always come in early. Do you recall hearing or seeing anything unusual?" Allemand kept tapping. "Are you okay, Royce? Can you put the pen down? It's distracting. What's wrong with you?"

Allemand paled as he tried to hide his reaction. "I'm fine. Just a little warm." The uneasiness lingered. So far, nobody seemed to suspect him. As luck would have it, Vick, the crew scheduler, had quit right after the crash. Vick said he didn't get paid enough to deal with the pressure from the intense scrutiny generated by the incident. Evidently, it hadn't occurred to Vick that Allemand might have slipped into his office and placed the call.

"No one on my staff has said a word to me," said Allemand. "I rarely leave my office at that time of the morning. Since I'm usually the only one around, there's no real need to be out and about. Like I told security, I had a meeting with Vick earlier that morning. Someone may have slipped by while we were together." He stopped himself there, worried that he might have said too much already.

He was glad he was wearing his suit jacket. He could feel the sweat drip down his chest and under his arms. He couldn't let Tony sense his anxiety. Was his plan backfiring? He needed to relax, play it cool. Too many open issues. He still didn't know how much more Bobby Cisco knew and where he might have hidden the evidence.

He was tormented. What kind of information could this Cantwell woman have gathered? He cursed to himself. He was haunted by his last conversation with Bobby. He had thought that, with Cisco out of the picture, his plans were safe. Now he wasn't so sure. He had to find a way to get his hands on Cisco's logbooks. "Tony, do you have those documents here? Perhaps we could take a look at them ourselves before you meet with Ms. Cantwell," Allemand commented, still sprawled out in the chair.

"No, Royce. Actually, Ms. Cantwell has the only copy. Unfortunately, our new paralegal didn't realize we didn't have copies, and she sent some of the originals off to Ms. Cantwell. I just found out and haven't had a chance to ask Ms. Cantwell if she'd mind making copies and sending our documents back. We usually have the originals, but the NTSB or FAA—I can't remember which—hasn't released them; they just forwarded a copy to us."

It took Allemand a few minutes to recover from the initial shock of possible exposure. He needed to do something stat. He wondered what Cisco could have put in the books. He couldn't have been stupid enough to mention details. He had to know that the government— or someone—would check those records at some point in his career. Nevertheless, Allemand had a sinking feeling in his gut. He had to see those logs. The brass ring was moving farther and farther from his grasp.

"Royce, enough about the Cisco case. Let's get back to the expansion project," Tony said, interrupting Allemand's thoughts.

Allemand looked at his watch. "I'm sorry, Tony. I just remembered. I have another appointment in ten minutes. Can we get back to the project later?" He stood up and straightened his jacket.

"Sure. My apologies for the interruption. Why don't you reschedule with my secretary, Joan?"

"Thanks, Tony. That Cisco case ..." Allemand paused. "Seems interesting, but strange. Good luck." He scurried from the room. Beads of perspiration oozed onto his forehead and upper lip and began to trickle down his face. He had to collect his thoughts and come up with a plan.

Chapter 14

Allemand's head ached. His throat tightened. He knew it. The nightmare was beginning.

He rushed back to his office to get his car keys, his mind running full speed ahead. I have to get out of here and get hold of Murillo. He's still in San Salvador. Can't call from my office. Can't risk using my cell.

He hurried outside. The gust of wind lifted a few strands of his hair from his lacquered coiffure. With a shaky hand, he attempted to put them in place.

Another dreary day with storms was predicted—the sky overcast, clouds green and ominous.

He sprinted to his reserved parking space close to the entrance of the building and got into his new black Lexus sedan. While driving down the street trying to figure out what to do, he spotted a gas station. A pay phone stood on a grassy patch a few yards from the pumps. He parked his car close to the booth and jumped out, the engine still running.

Damn it! He thought to himself, while he tried to circumnavigate a muddy hole that surrounded the phone. His temper escalated as he looked down to see his expensive handmade leather shoes squish into the murky puddle.

He looked up at the dark clouds that promised another heavy downpour. He pulled some coins from his pocket and tried to stick them in the slot. He pushed and pushed to no avail—the slot was blocked. He hit zero to get an operator. It rang and rang. "This is crazy," he said aloud. Finally an operator answered and he asked her to attempt a collect call to Murillo's private number. "Please work!" He tapped on the phone so hard he broke a nail on his middle finger. "Come on, answer the phone."

"*Hola*!" Murillo accepted the charges.

"I knew it! I just knew nothing good would come out of this!" Allemand shrieked. "I thought we resolved the Cisco threat, but we still have a problem."

"*Idiota*! You idiot! What are you talking about? How could there be a problem—he's dead."

"Cisco's wife is suing my company. She says the company forced him to come back to work so he flew in bad weather to get there on time. She claims that's why he got into the accident. Viscount hired some woman to act as an expert witness on their behalf. Evidently, she found some unusual remarks in his logbooks. It may not be anything, but I won't be able to rest until I know." He ran his fingers through his wet, greasy hair, messing it up even more.

He wished he had never agreed to get involved with Murillo; but the money had just been too much to resist. He began to worry about his own life ... his dreams. He longed for the day that he could cash it all in and move on with his goal to start his own airline. One day Murillo would let him out. He just had to find a way—and soon. Concern about exposure rattled his mind.

"Don't worry," said Murillo. "We will let Big Vern take care of it. Whatever it is, it couldn't be too obvious or the feds would be all over us by now."

"Just make sure he doesn't waste any time. I happen to know that this woman is going out of town tomorrow morning. Big Vern needs to get over to her house and get those documents. Her name is Josey Cantwell. Shouldn't be hard to find out where she lives." Allemand's voice was increasingly shrill. "Wait! Wait! Don't let him take the logbooks! Can he photograph them? We don't want anyone to suspect anything. If they find something missing, they might put things together. Or maybe we can just make it look like a robbery."

"Calm down, Royce. Vern will handle it. Don't worry. Vern will get the information."

The clouds opened up and rain poured down in buckets. Allemand ran back to his car, his Armani suit drenched. He jumped inside and sat, staring ahead, oblivious to his spattered clothing, the rain-soaked leather seats, or the mud stomped into the plush carpet.

He tilted the rearview mirror down and saw the image of a face he hardly recognized. It was pale and drawn. His slick, black hair fell in disarray around his face. Little droplets of water dangled like icicles from his eyebrows. For the first time since going into business with Murillo, he feared for his career, his dreams, and his life.

Chapter 15

The next day, Josey rose early, pulled out the Cisco files, and began to go through them again. "What's this?" She'd discovered a photocopy of a sticky note inserted into the pages of one of the logbooks. The note contained an address in Dallas—nothing else. "This is Bobby's handwriting. I wonder what the significance of this address is." His handwriting had a distinctive, feminine look. She figured Bobby had stuck the note there to remind him of something. She put the note next to the stack and continued to review the logbooks.

Rene walked into the room. "I'm ready to take you to the airport."

"I got so involved reading Cisco's logbooks, I lost track of time."

Josey had a nine-o'clock flight to Chicago to interview some of the employees at Benton Air. She wished Brad could be with her, but he had another commitment. He had briefed her on some of the questions he needed answered, and she would fill him in on the details in a couple of days.

"Rene, did you finish that PowerPoint presentation for the college seminar I'm conducting next week?"

"Uh-huh. It looks good. But, you'd better go over it once more before your speech. Come on, Mom, you need to get going."

Josey didn't mind Rene's mothering attitude. In fact, she knew she needed to be prompted. "I really need to finish reviewing these Cisco documents. There's a lot more information I need to cover. I'll take them with me on the airplane. Help me get these papers into my case." She started cramming the documents into a laptop bag that sported 180-degree rotating wheels. "My suitcase is already packed." She had a simple philosophy: she brought whatever she could remember and bought what she forgot—and she always forgot something. "Just grab the whole batch of what's left, and I'll try to sort it out along the way. To be honest, I'm finding this lawsuit pretty fascinating. The deeper I dig, the more bizarre it gets. By the time I get home, I should have a lot of compelling information to share with Tony McIntyre. I guess the company never looked at Cisco's flying records. They would've smoked him. The way I see it, he was an accident waiting to happen. Seemed like a rogue to me. I don't know how many pilots take the kinds of risks this character did, but

I can tell you, they sure don't document it."

"Remember you told me about the guy who documented his love life in his logbooks—like a steamy novel?" Rene asked.

"Yeah, the staff had a field day with that one—better than a soap opera. But that isn't typical. I've seen some weird stuff over the years though. Some of the reports read like fantasy." Josey leaned over to tie her shoes. "Imagine having 'Captain' Bobby Cisco on your flight. I can hear him now. 'Let's just fly right through the storm—tell the passengers to buckle up!' Did you ever see that cartoon with the pilots in the cockpit making the airplane bounce all over the sky while they're grinning like two kids in an arcade? I can visualize him in the cockpit."

"You're weird, Mom. Get a move on. Come on. You'll miss your flight."

"Okay, okay. I'm going," Josey said.

Together, they picked up Josey's bags and headed out. As the front door closed behind them, Rene asked, "Aren't you going to set the alarm?"

"Nah. Natasha is here. I'm sure she'll scare away any would-be intruders."

They got in Rene's car and took off for the Dallas/Fort Worth International Airport. Rene dropped Josey off at the terminal door closest to the departure gate. "So long. Good luck!" Rene yelled as her mother gathered her carry-on bags and hurried to the gate.

"Thanks for the ride, Rene. Take the rest of the day off."

"I might just do that," Rene said. "Love ya, Mom."

Josey made it to the gate just in time for the first boarding call. She waited for her row to be announced and wheeled her cart onto the MD-80 aircraft. She looked inside the cockpit and checked out the crew. Don't know them, she thought, and breathed a sigh of relief. Over the years, she had met a few unstable kooks who claimed to be pilots. Just in case she saw one in the cockpit, she wanted to have the chance to bail before takeoff. Her queasy stomach settled.

Her fear of flying had escalated after she'd heard about the Benton Air crash. The news media attention had caused apprehension among the traveling public; fearful passengers were canceling trips on small aircraft. Superstitious people would say these things happen in three's; maybe that would be the end of it. But that didn't take away her anxiety.

The NTSB had asked her and Brad to be on standby again. They thought it would be helpful to keep the same team in place in case they found a connection among the crashes. She didn't know if she could handle more work, and she revisited her regret about taking on the Cisco case.

The flight took off on time. She settled into the cramped coach seat in row eight next to a window; the adjacent seat was vacant. She clutched the armrests, her knuckles turning white as she endured the clear-air turbulence during the climb. Daring to look out the window, she watched the cities of Dallas and Fort Worth disappear below her, flat and still green from the recent rains. She missed the rolling hills and mountains of the East Coast where she had grown up.

The plane reached altitude and smoothed out. She let go of the armrest. After massaging her fingers for a few moments, she rummaged through her carry-on case, pulled out the Cisco logs, and continued reading.

She noticed Bobby alternated between flying the L-382 and the DC-8, but saw more charters listed. He'd flown at least one trip a week, and the majority of his flights were to South and Central America. If I ever want to know what to do in Central America, I know where to look, she thought, skimming over the names of hotels, restaurants, and other attractions that were jotted down in the remarks area.

She wondered if he had kept another clean edition of his logbook somewhere else. She couldn't imagine him handing this to an airline at an interview.

Here we go again—didn't he have anything better to do with his life? The initials RA and AM showed up several times on his flights. Who were these people? Maybe they were crew members or something. He seemed to see them often—perhaps girlfriends? Poor Annie. He didn't deserve her. He sure crammed a lot of detail into this little remarks area, she thought. I'd love to know what this stuff means. She thought about Bobby's death and all the loose ends he'd left. She noticed how he used initials on his business trips, but actual first names on his pleasure flights. Odd.

She reflected on her previous cases. Many turned out to be big mysterious puzzles, waiting to be unraveled. This one intrigued her most. Based upon Bobby's deceptive personality, her curiosity piqued even more curious of the activities he recorded. She dove in with determination to get to the core of those comments.

Josey could feel the aircraft descending. She glanced out the window. A sprawling metropolis emerged. She tightened her seatbelt and took in the skyline—so different from that of Dallas and Fort Worth.

She finished stuffing the papers back into her bag just as the flight pulled into the gate at Chicago O'Hare Airport.

AM and RA—Hmmm? I guess it will have to wait.

Chapter 16

After Allemand's panicked phone call, Murillo summoned his trusted stateside bodyguard and chauffeur, Big Vern. Vern had been a dedicated servant to Murillo for over fifteen years. Murillo overlooked some of his flaws, like his frustrating hearing problem, because Big Vern faithfully followed any command, regardless of the nature or the consequences. This had been demonstrated years ago when an enemy made an attempt on Murillo's life. Big Vern had rescued him, and in the process had suffered serious injuries to the left side of his head—leaving him almost deaf. Because of Vern's loyalty, Murillo had learned to deal with the man's weakness.

"You need to go to this Cantwell lady's house and get me some documents." Murillo handed Big Vern a slip of paper with an address written on it.

Big Vern, a big, burly man, stood six foot seven. His long salt-and-pepper hair circled around a bald spot on his head and was pulled back into a ponytail. His smooth, hairless facial skin denoted a hint of Native American heritage. The name "Big" definitely fit—but no one knew where the "Vern" had originated.

"Say again?" Big Vern answered.

Murillo, holding back his frustration, repeated himself. "I told you. Go to this house. I need you to photograph Bobby Cisco's flying records." He explained exactly what they looked like. "Okay? Have I made it clear? And make sure you are not seen."

Vern understood.

—✦—

The brilliant sun had just peeked over the horizon when Big Vern arrived at Josey's house. He drove a paneled utility truck with no markings. Josey's red brick house stood on a cul-de-sac abutted by an easement in the back and two vacant lots on the left. Josey owned the lot on the right, which provided her with additional privacy.

Big Vern attracted no attention as he parked on the cul-de-sac adjacent to the other vacant lot. Maintenance vehicles in that area were common.

He watched Josey through the rear view mirror as she threw her bags into Rene's car.

His eyes followed the car until it was well out of sight. He waited a few minutes longer to make sure they didn't return.

Daytime break-ins presented some risks, but Vern always followed his orders, and he didn't see anyone out and about. His surveillance the day before had revealed that most of the people in Josey's area worked during the day. Her backyard was fenced in, and it backed up to one of several vineyards in Texas.

To avoid attention, he had dressed like a nondescript maintenance person, his head covered with a UT Austin baseball cap lowered close to his eyes. Dark tinted aviator glasses completed the disguise. He opened the side gate, casually strolled into the yard, and walked up to the back of the house.

Surprised that the door was unlocked, he entered the house through the sliding glass door that led into Josey's bedroom. It took no time to find the office, and he quickly set about his task to search for files that referenced Cisco.

He'd been instructed to photograph any documents that looked like personal property of Cisco and then get out. With the skill of a practiced thief, he sifted through the documents on Josey's desk.

He found some of the Cisco documents right away, but he didn't see anything that looked like logbooks or personal records.

Totally immersed in his task, he didn't hear the front door open.

— ✦ —

Rene had inadvertently left her cell phone at Josey's, so on her way home, she'd decided to go back to the house to pick it up. She walked through the small quiet rooms to the kitchen where she remembered leaving the phone on the island.

What sounded like paper shuffling directed her attention toward Josey's office. While on trips, her mother usually left the door to the office shut to keep Luc out. The cat had a fondness for jumping on the desk and messing up her important documents. "I hope Luc hasn't created another big mess on Mom's desk for me to clean up." She let out a soft mumble.

She walked to the office and found the door ajar, just as she figured. "Luc? You in here again?" Rene called out. She swung open the door and directed her attention to the desk.

Big Vern turned around and stood face to face with her.

Rene was shocked when she saw the vision of the green Hulk—minus the green—before her. "What the hell ..." but before she could finish the sentence, Big Vern grabbed her, picked her up like a rag doll, and flung her against the wall. Her head hit with a thud, and she slithered to the floor, where she lay dazed.

After a moment, she struggled to get up, but he came at her again. She heard a crack and felt a sharp pain in her right shoulder. Falling the second time, she hit the credenza with a strong jolt, causing a large picture of the Blue Angel's flying team to fall from the wall, missing her by mere inches.

Rene tried to focus her eyes on her attacker. The hat and dark reflective glasses kept her from getting a clear picture of him before he ran out of the house. The light slowly dimmed as she slipped into unconsciousness.

—◆—

Hearing some sort of ruckus coming from the main house, Natasha ran out of the garage apartment, just missing a personal encounter with Big Vern as he took off in the truck. She memorized the license plate number and took notice as much as she could of the truck's description.

Natasha found Rene still unconscious on the floor, blood dripping from the side of her head. She remembered seeing a first aid kit in the kitchen, and in no time she had assessed Rene's condition, bound her head, and with great care, had pulled some pillows off the sofa and laid them around Rene to cushion her and keep her from moving.

—✦—

Rene awoke, stunned and in pain from the slam against the wall. She saw Natasha leaning over her. "What happened? How long have I been out?" She touched the gauze that was wrapped around her head, blood still trickling through the light fabric.

"You will be fine. I called 911. Please stay quiet. You were bleeding. Try not to move—you might have a broken shoulder and concussion."

Rene looked up at Natasha. "Oh my God. I thought he was going to kill me." She tried to move, but Natasha made her stay put until the paramedics got there.

"I need to call my husband," Rene said. She looked helplessly toward the phone, which had fallen off the desk in the scuffle.

"I call him already. He is on the way," Natasha said.

"Oh, Natasha, you are amazing. Thank you."

"Of course."

—◆—

The police, paramedics, and Adam arrived within minutes of each other. While the police started marking off the scene, the paramedics unloaded the stretcher.

Adam ran inside first to find his wife crouched against the wall surrounded by cushions, her face cringed with pain. "Rene, what happened?" Adam's voiced trembled. "You're hurt!"

Rene looked up at him, still rigid from fear. Seeing her husband and knowing she was safe caused the floodgates to release. Her body relaxed, and she sobbed with abandon.

Adam crouched down close to Rene and put his arm around her, careful not to put pressure on the sensitive spots.

The paramedics came into the room. "Sir," one of them said gently to Adam, "you're going to have to get out of the way so we can check her out."

"It's my shoulder. I can't move it." She let out a shriek as the paramedic lifted her shoulder and gently let it drop. "He threw me against the wall—I blacked out. He was so strong." Rene's voice weakened.

"She needs to get to the hospital and get that x-rayed," the paramedic said. "She has some serious bruises too. Look at her head—that's a pretty nasty cut and bump. We need to check for a concussion, and we can't be sure if there are any internal injuries."

The paramedic looked up at Rene's husband and Natasha and the police officers who were convening on the scene. "We need to get her to the ER."

The police interrupted and started questioning Rene about the break-in. She told them all she could remember about the man. "He was huge and strong." She had no problem remembering that part about her attacker. "He was so huge!" Rene repeated. "J—just a minute," she stammered, "I remember ... I do think I saw hair hanging down his back—gray. He had a long, gray ponytail. I think he was old. And he wore gloves. I could tell when he grabbed me." She looked at Adam for reassurance and then looked at Natasha, who was standing quietly to the side. "I'm so glad Natasha was here to help."

Adam looked at Natasha. "Thanks so much. Your quick response may have saved her life."

Natasha nodded and gave the police officers the description of the van and the license number.

"We'll do the best we can," the officer said, "but we wish you had a better description of him.

Rene said she had never even noticed the van when she got back to the house.

While the police and paramedics continued to question Rene, Adam called Rene's brother, Cary. "Come right away," Adam said, his voice urgent. "Rene's been hurt. They're going to take her to the hospital."

"What happened? Is it serious?" Cary asked. Even though he had teased his twin sister relentlessly when they were growing up, they still had that bond that others couldn't understand. At times, they almost seemed to have a psychic link, sensing each other's joy and pain.

"I think she'll be okay. Someone broke into your mom's house. He attacked Rene. I'll tell you about it when you get here. Can you come to her house right away?" Adam said. He hung up without waiting for Cary's answer and ran back to Rene.

"Did you call Brad?" Adam asked Rene.

"Not yet."

Natasha approached them. "I already call Brad. He is coming now."

"I don't want to get in that ambulance," Rene cried.

"It's okay. It's best," Adam reassured her. "We don't know how badly you're hurt. Just get in. I'll follow in the car. I promise."

Cary, just minutes away, arrived while the paramedics were coercing Rene to let them put her in the ambulance—she hated hospitals. All she could think of was the phrase everyone used when referring to the one they were taking her. "Once you go into DFH, you never come out."

Adam briefed Cary on what had happened.

"What about Mom?" Rene asked Cary.

"Don't worry about Mom. I'll call her—you just get going."

"Go with Rene, Adam. I'll stay here with the police," Cary insisted, putting his arm around Adam's shoulder, consoling him while he walked him to his car.

Against her will, Rene finally allowed herself to be wheeled into the ambulance, which left immediately for the hospital. Adam followed.

—◆—

The lights and noise of the police cars and ambulance drew the attention of the few neighborhood people who were at home. They inched toward the house to investigate the commotion.

One of the police officers approached the small crowd to see if anyone had noticed anything suspicious or any vehicles parked nearby. Nobody had.

Cary led the police through the house. Nothing seemed disturbed except the files on Josey's desk. One of the officers told Cary to have Josey check everything when she got home to see if anything was missing.

When the police finally took off, Cary headed back into the house. Natasha had disappeared. He dreaded the call to his mother.

As he was about to go into the house, Brad pulled up and jumped out of the car. "Cary, I got here as quick as I could. How is Rene?"

"Thanks, Brad. She'll be okay, but I can use your support right now."

"Have you called Josey?"

"No, I'm getting up my nerve."

They walked into the house together. Cary walked over to the wine rack and pulled out one of his mom's fine Merlots. "I know it's early, but I need something to relax me a little. Mom is going to freak out. You know how she is with us."

Brad smiled. "Let me have one too."

After pouring two hefty glasses and handing one to Brad, Cary lowered himself onto the sofa, took a deep breath, swallowed a big gulp of the wine, and dialed Josey's cell phone number.

Chapter 17

"Let's take a quick break," remarked Dr. Mack Wagner, one of the NTSB investigators on the Benton Air case. He and Josie had been interviewing some of the flight operations managers and check airmen—pilots who are assigned to make sure the pilots meet FAA and company standards. After the interviews, the next step would be to look at training records.

"It's looking more and more like pilot error to me," said Mack. "But something else seems wrong—I just can't put my finger on it."

"There doesn't seem to be any love lost for Captain Daine, that's for sure," Josey added. "From what we keep hearing around here, it seems that nobody wanted to fly with him."

"Some say he had a heart attack," Mack said. "Several of the employees seemed surprised because, although he was a big man, he appeared to be in such good physical shape. But hey, with the kind of attitude and temper he apparently displayed, who knows? Stranger things have happened. Lou was young and new, but everyone said he was a natural and an excellent stick," Mack continued.

"What about the Orleans Air Cargo accident in New Orleans? " Josey enquired. "Have you heard anything on that one yet?" She knew Mack had been working on that case too. In fact, he had been at the crash site right after the plane went down.

"Nothing yet, Josey. Hope you have some free time." He smiled knowing that Josey was longing for more free time—for herself, not work.

Josey groaned and made a face. It was so hard for her to say no to an assignment.

Mack and Josey started walking to the next office when her cell phone rang. It was Cary.

"Excuse me a minute, Mack," Josey said.

"Mom, where are you?"

"Cary, what's up? I'm in Chicago. I thought you knew that."

"Yeah, I know—I just meant are you able to talk?"

"I'm on my way to another meeting. What's wrong?" Josey's instincts were kicking in. She could always tell when Cary was upset.

—◆—

He didn't want to worry his mother, but had to tell her something. He cut right to the chase. "Someone broke into your house." Without taking a breath so his mother couldn't interrupt, he continued. "Rene came back by the house to pick up her phone and caught the guy in the act. He threw her against the wall before he fled the house." He tried to downplay her injuries. He'd wait to see what the doctors found out. "She's got a few bruises, but she'll be okay."

"Let me talk to her," Josey said. Her first concern was the welfare of her daughter.

"Well, actually she went to the hospital. Just to be on the safe side," Cary continued, trying to take his mother's mind off Rene. "We can't tell if he had anything with him when he ran out. The papers on your desk are all a mess. We can't tell what he might have been looking for. What do you think he was after? What could you have that was so important that someone would actually break into your house to steal it?" he asked.

"Look, right now all I care about is Rene. I need to get home right away. We'll worry about those other things later. Did you call the police?"

"Of course. They just left. I'm not sure what they can do. Nothing seems to be missing. The intruder was wearing gloves, so there were no fingerprints on anything. Mom, I agree. You need to get home."

"I'm going to call the airline now and see how quickly I can get a flight home. Hang up and I'll call you back as soon as I take care of the arrangements. You can pick me up at the airport, and we'll figure out what to do as soon as I get home."

"Mom, why don't you stay with me? The intruder might come back."

"We'll see, Cary. We can discuss it when I get home. Did you call Brad?"

"Actually, he is right here."

"Let me talk to him."

Cary handed the phone to Brad. "Josey, everything is going to be okay. Just get on home. I promise we'll get to the bottom of this."

"Okay. What about Natasha? Was she home?"

"She heard the noise and ran inside, but missed the intruder. She took care of Rene until Adam got there. She was able to get the license plate and a description of the van, but I'm sure it will lead us nowhere."

—◆—

Josey punched the end button and turned to face Mack.

"Josey, you're pale. What was that all about?" Mack had been anxious for her to hang up so he could find out what was going on.

"My house was broken into. Some brute assaulted Rene, but thank God she wasn't hurt too badly. At least I don't think she was— Cary was a little vague about it. I can't imagine why these things keep happening to me. I was just getting over the recent fire when that creep from the lawsuit tried to kill me. Why can't it be just little stuff with me? It's always something big. Do other people experience as many catastrophes or is it just me?" Josey said wearily. "I need to get back home, Mack. I'm sorry. You'll just have to tell me what you discover. Let me know if I need to come back. Otherwise, I expect to be back in town in a couple of months."

"Josey, I understand. It's not a problem. Be careful. I've known you for over ten years now, and you're right—sometimes you draw trouble like a magnet." Mack tried to lighten the conversation to ease her tension.

Josey smiled. She hadn't expected Mack to agree with her.

The airline had a flight leaving at six in the evening. Josey made the change to her ticket and phoned Cary back with the details.

During the entire trip home, her mind was filled with thoughts of Rene and the break-in. She kept trying to figure out what she had in her house that was so important. Since nothing seemed to be missing, Josey began to wonder if she might have in her possession whatever it was the intruder had wanted.

She was glad Brad was there. He always helped her keep things in perspective, plus she could use a strong shoulder to lean on this time.

She sighed and pulled out the Cisco files. She sensed that somehow the burglary might be connected to this case. "I need to figure this out," she said. The passengers seated nearby glanced over as she realized she'd been talking to herself.

Rene was always saying that her mother had a sixth sense. Josey often predicted things that actually happened. Although it was probably just a coincidence, it happened enough that Rene respected her mother's gut feelings, and now Josey's gut feeling was telling her that this case was trouble.

Josey found it increasingly difficult to concentrate. She finally put the papers back into her case and sat quietly for the remainder of the trip, staring out the window into the darkness surrounding the airplane.

The kids were right, Josey was thinking. It was time to back off and retire. Yes, that's what she was going to do. She closed her eyes, arching her stiff neck and shoulders against the headrest on the seat. Yes, she told herself again. When all this is over, I'll stop taking on any more cases.

Chapter 18

"The documents weren't there," Murillo explained over the phone to Allemand. Murillo was calm and deliberate, smoking his Cuban cigar and watching the smoke drift across the patio of his mansion in San Salvador where he was enjoying his first cup of coffee of the day. Murillo explained what had happened between Big Vern and Rene.

—◆—

"What do you mean not there? Did he find anything?" Allemand was out of his mind with rage. He paced back and forth in his study at home in Dallas. "I know she has them. We have got to find out what's in those logbooks!" He hadn't slept well since his discovery in Tony McIntyre's office. His eyes were sunken, his clothes disheveled. An ash from his cigarette fell on his silk shirt, burning a small, uneven hole in the expensive fabric. Allemand just flicked the spot with his thumb and middle finger, oblivious to the damage to his shirt.

"There were some files relating to the case, but no logbook copies," Murillo said. "She must have taken them with her. Big Vern thinks he saw everything before he got out. He insists the documents weren't there."

"That idiot! Don't you think the Cantwell woman will be suspicious since the daughter saw Vern going through the documents on her desk?" Allemand shouted.

There was a pause. Allemand remembered Murillo's affection for Big Vern and tried to recover his composure. "Sorry, I wasn't trying to insult your man, Vern. I'm just letting off steam."

—✦—

Murillo continued, his voice more haughty than usual, "She couldn't possibly know what he was looking for. Nothing was taken, and no one knows how long he was there before the girl came back to the house."

"Look, Royce"—Murillo was getting irritated with Allemand's attitude—"I'm telling you, we'll get the logs. Maybe it's nothing. How can anyone link this burglary to us? It's impossible. I told you, if she had any idea what we were doing, we wouldn't be sitting here talking right now." He continued: "I'm leaving for Dallas tonight and flying into Addison Airport in my jet. Meet me in the morning. We'll talk about it then."

"I can't take any chances." Allemand's voice was terse. "We have to get hold of those documents. Keep your men after it. Do whatever it takes to get the records. If that Cantwell woman has any clue at all about what we're doing ... well, we just can't let anything happen."

"Don't worry, I said. This is minor stuff. You're overreacting," Murillo interjected. He was getting sick of this wimp. Allemand had known what the score was when he got into the business. It would be so easy to eliminate him, and that thought had crossed his mind more than once. But he needed Allemand to handle the transportation end. Everything to date was running like clockwork. Just perfect.

Chapter 19

Cary met Josey at the airport, and together they drove straight to the hospital. Cary made an attempt at small talk, but Josey wouldn't have it. "What was he looking for that would be so important that he would assault Rene?" she asked. "The only case I'm working on now is the Cisco one. It had to be that."

"Mom, stop getting yourself so worked up. Brad will get to the bottom of this."

"I'm glad we're here," Cary said when they reached the hospital. They left the car at the valet stand and rushed inside. Adam had already called with the room number, and they headed that way.

As Josey and Carey entered the room, Adam got up from his chair next to Rene's bed. "The doctor wants to observe Rene for a while longer just to be on the safe side," he said. "She hit her head pretty hard as you can see from the big knot. She also cut her head—took ten stitches." Adam pointed to the bandage on Rene's head.

Josey stared at the knot. It looked about the size of a golf ball. "Oh, Rene. Look at you. You're so pale. I can't believe that thug. Are you okay? I've been so worried." Josey's words tumbled out.

"I'll be okay. I guess. My shoulder is fractured. The ER doctor said all they can do is put my arm in a sling for now. Other than that, just a bump, a few bruises, and the cut. They're going to let me go home soon. Don't worry. I'm fine." She took her mother's hand. "Mom, don't stay home by yourself. Go home with Cary or have him stay at your house. Promise me," she pleaded.

"Yeah, yeah—okay," Josey said. It was tearing her up to see her daughter like this, battered and bruised, an IV dripping into her arm.

Cary drove Josey back to her house. It was late, and they were both tired. Neither one of them said much in the car. Josey's anxiety level was high as she walked to the front door. "Knowing some stranger rummaged through my stuff gives me an eerie feeling." She dreaded that first step over the threshold. She went into the office. A wave of nausea overtook her as she surveyed the area.

"I left everything as it was so you can take a look to see if anything appears to be missing." Cary said.

"The police said he came into the house through your bedroom. The sliding door was still slightly open, but they couldn't find any fingerprints. They're going to keep an eye on the place for a while, but you know that won't last long," Cary said as he stood by the door.

"This is weird, but I still think the intruder was somehow interested in the Cisco records," Josey said. "Bobby was keeping track of something in his logbooks, but what? I need to get to the bottom of this mystery if it is the last thing I do."

"Mom, maybe so, but I'm really worried about you. Why don't you stay at my place for a while?"

"I'll be okay, Cary. I have double locks and a good security system. You saw to that after the Ashton case. If I hear so much as a cricket chirp, I'll call right away. And don't forget, Natasha is here now."

"Some security system. You need to use it," he said sarcastically. "I'll stay tonight and probably tomorrow, and then we'll see." He still wouldn't be dissuaded. "Rene was lucky that the guy didn't hurt her any worse."

Cary settled down in the living room to watch TV, and Josey went into her bedroom to change out of her business clothes into some comfortable sweats. She walked over to the sliding glass door and opened it. A chill went through her thinking that someone had entered her bedroom. She stepped outside and looked around. It had been too easy for the intruder. She looked at the fence and decided to get a lock for her gate first thing the next day.

As Josey was stepping back into the house, she spotted a cigarette butt on the concrete deck near the door. She picked it up and went inside, walking back to the living room.

"Cary, I found this cigarette butt in the backyard by my door. It probably came from the intruder. Maybe I should tell the police."

"It could be Natasha's."

"No, hers are different. Plus I don't believe Natasha would drop a cigarette butt in the yard."

"Good idea, Mom. But let's wait until morning."

Josey went into the kitchen and pulled out a sandwich bag from the cabinet. She dropped the butt inside. Just as she was about to turn and carry it back into her office, Natasha entered the kitchen through the back door carrying a large bag. Josey watched in awe as the strange woman pulled out an amazing array of meats, cheeses, and olives and displayed them on the counter next to a warm loaf of focaccia bread. "I bring food. Now eat!"

"I don't think I'm hungry," said Josey meekly.

"You will be." Natasha pushed the food closer.

"I can eat." Cary walked into the kitchen and started filling a plate.

Once Josey started eating, she couldn't stop. Natasha's food was like ambrosia. She wondered where she had learned her flair for food—and her perfect timing. "Okay," she said after a while. "I'm stuffed. I'm going into the office to see if I can find any clues to what someone was so anxious to retrieve." It was getting late, but Josey couldn't rest. "It's got to be here. I've been over these logbooks twice." She needed to unravel the mystery before something more serious happened.

She opened the music media file on her PC, clicked on her easy listening playlist, and reached for a match to light a couple of the vanilla-scented candles she kept on her desk. The gentle music and calming scents would fill the office and created a mental warmth and serenity. What would put anyone else to sleep made Josey more effective. Once the candles were glowing, she started going through the documents for the third time.

But lighting the match had reminded her about the discarded cigarette butt she had found in the back. A light went on. "Of course, the cigarette!" Josey picked up the little plastic bag and opened it. As she brought the cigarette butt up for a closer look, the fading, but familiar, scent drifted up to her nose. That smell. She thought hard. The cigarette brought up recollections. Josey remembered.

"Cary! Look here!" she called as she walked quickly into the living room.

"What?" He jumped up, turned, and ran smack into Josey as she approached the sofa.

"This is the same kind of cigarette that Annie Cisco was smoking. I'm sure of it. I remember the gold stripe around the end and the distinctive nasty smell. If this was from the guy who broke in, we might have a link that proves there is more to the Cisco case than meets the eye. It's got to be in these logs!" She rushed back into her office and plunged into the records with a renewed vigor. Papers flew as she anxiously tried to find the pages that documented Cisco's flights to San Salvador. Cary picked up a few of the papers. "Look for DFW—SAL."

"Calm down, Mom. It's going to take you longer when you flip through randomly like that. Just slow down and check each page."

"Here it is. Look here. Check this out!" She read from the log book: 'Feb 5–DFW-SAL.' See the remarks? 'AM and RA—La Taverna del Sol. Feb 14—DFW- SAL—bossman and AM again— same joint. 5 pax to flt-lp TKY023. Mar 11— similar notes—6 pax to flt, same LP.'" Calmer now, she put the pages down, flopped onto the sofa, and looked at her son. "What do you think this means? Do you think he means passengers? LP?"

"There could be a connection here, Mom. How many times do you see this?"

Josey picked up the bag holding the cigarette again, careful not to touch it. "We need to find out where these cigarettes come from. It might be a long shot. How can this help us other than the fact that we know the culprit might have a tie to someone in San Salvador? We can give it to the police to check for fingerprints, but get real—we'll never find the person. Could be someone from Viscount too. Why would they care? They have the same information I have. There must be a connection here." She put the bag down. "This case is starting to make me nervous." Josey shuddered. "Cisco was watching these people. I wonder if he was stalking one of them? Maybe he was mad at his boss. Wonder what they did to him? I hope I'm not opening up a can of worms."

"Now I really believe you're letting your imagination go wild," Carey said.

"I'm calling Brad. If anyone can find out, he can do it," Josey said as she rushed to the phone.

"Don't you think you should call Viscount and tell them what's going on?" Cary asked, reminding his mother that they were the ones who had got her involved in this.

"Yes, I know. I can't help but feel that something odd is going on. Let's wait until we speak to Brad."

"It's really getting late. Let's wait to call Brad. There's nothing he can do right now. You have to be exhausted; I am. Let's go to bed and look at it again in the morning with fresh heads." Cary nudged his mom, and she relented, getting up and making her way to the bedroom.

Chapter 20

After a fitful night, Josey arose at 5:30 with only one thought on her mind. She wanted to call Brad first thing and let him know what she had learned and what she had been thinking. She already knew he was going to be mad for not calling the previous night.

—◆—

Brad saw Josey's name flash on the caller ID and, though groggy, he answered. "Josephine? What time is it?"

"Brad!" She ignored the "Josephine."

"Huh?"

"Get up! I need your help!"

"For someone who claims to be so independent, you can't seem to do anything without calling me first. What's up?" Brad yawned loudly and stretched as he positioned the phone between his shoulder and cheek.

"Can you come over?

"Is Rene okay?"

"Yes, I suppose so. I haven't heard anything new since last night. I got home late. Cary was all worked up over what happened and insisted on staying with me. I think it all has to do with the Cisco case I'm working on, and I'm pretty sure that I stumbled onto some information that will help clear this up. I really need you to help me. Can you come over right away? I'll fix you some breakfast, and we can go over everything."

"Tell you what. Get Natasha to fix breakfast, and I'll be there in twenty minutes."

"What's wrong with my cooking?"

"Come on—you've eaten her food."

Josey couldn't argue that point. "I don't want to wake her. She still scares me a little."

No sooner had Josey ended the call than she heard some noise in the kitchen. "Is this woman psychic or what?" Josey walked into the kitchen to see Natasha in her standard dark turtleneck shirt and the coveted amulet. Boris was standing guard next to her right leg. Luc ran over to Josey, hid behind her, and started hissing.

—◆—

As promised, Brad was there in twenty minutes looking as if he'd just got out of bed. He stood in the foyer wearing an old pair of jogging shorts and a T-shirt with a picture of a pig wearing binoculars.

"Well, you could have combed your hair," Josey remarked. "I wasn't dying!" They habitually talked to each other as if they were married. Cary and Rene always laughed at the way they treated each other. Pity they couldn't live with each other. The kids really liked Brad.

"I brushed my teeth. Where's breakfast?"

"In a minute. Natasha is working on it." Josey didn't pause. She grabbed Brad's arm and directed him into her office. Immediately, she began going over the details of the mystery. Brad, what do you make of this?" She picked up the pages of the logbook and handed them to him. "Not many clues. Do you know anyone down in Central America who can check out some of this?"

"Slow down, Josey. Let me take a good look." Brad, an experienced pilot and mechanic, flopped down onto Josey's chair and focused carefully on the documents. He had acquired his mechanic's license because he loved working on airplanes. Over the years he'd found it came in handy more than a few times. He kept his licenses current and flew small airplanes now and then. He was always coaxing Josey to go flying with him, but she wouldn't do it. She was deathly afraid of small airplanes, even when she really knew the pilots.

Brad continued to study the logs. Josey paced back and forth, anxious to get his feedback. She suddenly stopped. "See those initials, Brad? Who do you think they are?"

"Hey. Calm down. You're making me nervous. Go help Natasha. I'm starved." When she didn't move, he said, "I wonder if the burglar found what he was searching for." Thinking aloud, as he perused the logbooks, he said. "LP with numbers behind it—that could be a license plate. I'll check it out." He wrote down the information.

Josey knew how irritating it was for someone to look over her shoulder while she was trying to read something. She pouted and went to the kitchen to see if she could help and maybe pick up some of Natasha's cooking secrets. It would keep her occupied for a while.

"You could wake the dead, Mom." Cary came into the kitchen, looking just as bad as Brad. "Is Brad already here?"

"Yes. I couldn't wait. He'll know what to do."

At that moment, Brad joined them in the kitchen. "I think you're right, Josey." He sat down at the table to a lavish breakfast of eggs Benedict and a fruit plate. "There seems to be some kind of theme here—the flights, the cigarette butts. The notations seem consistent with someone tracking someone or something. I'll make some calls. I believe you're also right about this Cisco guy. It definitely looks like he was up to something."

"Mom, you're getting too involved again. It may not be your business. Why not turn it over to the Viscount people. Or better yet, the police." Cary, as usual, was trying to keep his mother out of danger.

"It is my business now. Someone broke into my house. How can I feel safe when I'm not sure who's responsible?"

"Josey, just stay put while I check this out. I mean it." This was a message frequently relayed by Brad. "Please listen to me this time."

"Yeah, yeah," mumbled Josey.

Having done justice to his food, Brad stood up. "I'm going to go over some of the other depositions and see if anyone with the initials

RA shows up. If I don't find anything, I'll call Tony. He's expecting to hear from me soon." He walked to the door, but turned back. "Listen, not to change the subject, but while you were gone I found out something interesting. First, remember the contract maintenance company A&P Contracting Services that worked on Benton Air? Well, it turns out that they've been under investigation for using faulty parts. Their license is on the verge of being suspended. Guess what else? What company do you think worked on the airplane that crashed in Florida?"

"Let me guess—A&P Contracting Services?" Josey chided.

"Right. And guess who the mechanic was on all three planes?"

"That guy who worked on the Benton Air airplane?"

"Right again. Chuck Finley!"

"That's incredible. Do you think you're on to something or is it just a coincidence?"

"The NTSB is checking it out. They still haven't found anything out of sorts, but this is opening up an intense investigation. We should have something soon."

Josey walked Brad to the door and watched as he got in his car and took off.

—◆—

Brad was still concerned about Josey. He decided it was time to call in his old gang from the CIA. He knew they had the skills and resources he needed to help him figure out who had broken into Josey's house. He knew it was a long shot. The details were sketchy. The person who broke in was definitely a pro.

Chapter 21

After Brad left, Josey went straight back into her office. She shuffled the papers on her desk, checked her e-mails, responded to a few, and played a couple of games of solitaire. When she got stressed, sometimes it took her a while to focus.

Okay, settle down, she thought as she pulled out the deposition given by one of the Viscount crew members who had been called on behalf of Annie Cisco.

As she neatly stacked the documents, she noticed the paper with the address on it that she'd earlier tossed aside. She checked the Bates number, an identification number that's given to each exhibit relating to a deposition. She went through the logbook pages until she came to the page in that sequence. The note was stuck to a page that included some of the odd remarks that had been documented during the San Salvador trips.

Being too strung out to read any more, Josey got on the Internet and googled the address written on the note that appeared to be stuck on the page—1221 Wale Park Avenue. It wasn't far. Maybe twenty minutes—thirty tops. She knew the area. It was mainly a hospital district, with several specialty hospitals and a variety of medical centers. She remembered her "miracle friend" who'd been in a hospital near there a few years previously. Josey had spent many days driving back and forth to visit her as she was recovering from a serious, life-threatening aneurysm. Not even the doctors thought she'd survive, but by the grace of God, she did, and she had continued on to live a blessed life with no lingering complications.

"It won't hurt to take a look," she told herself. "I'm just going to drive by. No harm in checking. Might give us another clue." As usual, Josey was trying to rationalize her need to plunge herself deeper into her work, oblivious to the risks.

She typed the address into her phone and replaced the original page on top of the other pages so she wouldn't disrupt the sequence of the documents.

Cary wandered in having gone off to shower after breakfast. "Cary, I'm going to run to the store. You want anything?"

"No thanks."

"Why don't you go on home? I'll be fine. I'm sure Brad will be over later." She didn't want to worry Cary. She knew that, if Cary had any idea she was going off to investigate, he'd probably tie her to a chair to keep her home.

"Okay. I'll go home and check my mail. I'll check back with you later today. I'm still planning to stay here for a few more days, you know."

Like Brad, Josey had her own Mercedes, only it was a luxury M Class SUV, desert silver metallic, her only true extravagance—her big splurge. Her favorite pastime was taking rides just for the sheer pleasure of driving it.

She plugged the address into her GPS, headed east, and found the area in Dallas with no problem. She slowed down to a crawl as she passed the building. It was a one-story brick building with little décor and was surrounded by a tall fence designed to keep out intruders. She noted there were very few windows. The gate was open.

Josey couldn't tell anything from the outward appearance of the building, so she decided to go inside and see what she could find out. She parked her car. Walking through the main entrance of the building, she found herself in what appeared to be a lobby. She looked for a directory but couldn't find one. What she had also failed to notice were the cameras positioned at various points in the lobby and in the parking lot.

It was difficult to tell from the lobby what kind of business was conducted here. Josey couldn't leave without at least knowing what they did. It could lead her to the reason for Bobby's notes. The lobby was void of furniture, but there was one small alcove. Walking nearer, she found that it sheltered a door with no sign. She was surprised when she turned the handle and found it unlocked. She walked in. She was amazed to see a luxurious waiting area. She didn't know much about brands of furniture, but she could tell the furnishings were very expensive. To the left of the entry was a sitting area in the corner that consisted of an elegant beige leather sofa with button back and a matching love seat, both set around a glass coffee table. Sitting on the table was a single issue of Robb Report magazine. Straight before her was a single cherrywood kidney-shaped desk with a leather top occupied by a solitary woman dressed in a crisp, formal, old-fashioned, nurse's uniform. The woman was concentrating on entering information into a computer.

Josey came to the conclusion it must be a clinic of some kind. Maybe Bobby was sick or the guy he was following was sick.

"Excuse me," Josey said, trying to be polite as she interrupted the nurse. "I think I might be in the wrong building. I'm looking for the Midtown Oncology Center. I can't find any directories in the building. I left the address at home, and my memory doesn't always come through for me. I thought this was the building."

"Sorry." The woman was polite, but brusque. "Nothing like that here. I can't help you."

"Oh, I'm so sorry to bother you. Wow—this place is really plush. You must cater to the rich and famous. What kind of medicine do your doctors practice?"

"Critical care," she said just as another woman, also in a nurse's uniform, entered the room from a side door and handed her a file. It was clear to Josey that she had been dismissed.

Before she left, she glanced through the open doorway to see a long hallway with several doors, each with a gold nameplate on it. The only one she could see clearly had the name Dr. Simon Winter printed on it. She filed the name away hoping she would remember it later. It might help her discover more about the clinic.

Josey went out of the building and climbed back into her car. She looked around the parking lot, unable to tell much by the cars parked there. There were several vans with handicap tags dangling from the rearview mirrors.

She just sat there for a few minutes. "Critical care?" Now she was really bewildered. Maybe Bobby really had been sick. He'd been so young. She figured it didn't really matter; he was dead anyway. "Oh my," Josey said aloud. "That was callous. I can't believe I just thought that."

Josey turned on the ignition and pulled out of the parking space. As she left the lot, she did notice a small emblem on the driver's door on one of the vans. It looked like a caduceus medical symbol. She could hardly distinguish the two snakes wrapped around the wing-tipped staff, but she was pretty sure that's what it was.

— ◆ —

Inside the building, a security guard sat at a desk surrounded by monitors that were linked to all the cameras inside and outside the building. The clinic was equipped with the latest advancements in security technology, and the camera feed was monitored twenty-four hours a day.

The guard watched Josey as she walked into

the clinic and again as she visited with the receptionist. He captured her picture on the computer screen and saved it to a file labeled "unknown visitors." Then he printed off a copy and set it aside. Could be nothing, but he decided to keep it handy in case he saw her again.

Chapter 22

As Josey was driving home from the clinic, her mind was churning a hundred different ways as she tried to piece things together. Nothing really made sense, but she had a feeling of uneasiness that she couldn't wipe from her mind. What were they really doing at the clinic? It all seemed so mysterious. Typical Josey ... her mind always suspicious.

As she drove, Josey called the hospital and spoke to Rene. She found out they were releasing her soon so there was no need for her to stop by. She headed straight home.

The phone was ringing as Josey walked into the house. It was Brad.

"Have you found out anything, Brad?"

"I'm still checking. The only thing I've been able to dig up so far is that the cigarettes we found were made in El Salvador. Maybe this all has to do with illegal transport. The unemployment rate in that country is out of control. People would do just about anything to get to the States. I don't know how this is connected to Cisco, but it makes sense to follow up." When Josie didn't respond immediately, he continued, "Are you okay? Do you want me to come over? Have you seen Rene?"

"Rene is going home soon, and I'm fine," Josey finally said. "I just want to be alone for a while to think things out. Somehow I don't think anyone will break into my home again in broad daylight."

"You mean like someone just did?" The remark was a bit sarcastic, but not biting.

"I'll call you later, Brad. Let me know as soon as you learn more," Josey said, dismissing his comment.

Josey didn't say anything to him about the clinic. It seemed so far-fetched that there would even be a connection that she decided to wait until she could come up with more clues. Maybe she could check with Tony at Viscount and see if Bobby had any friends or family who were critically ill. That might resolve the clinic matter. She decided to call Brad later.

She jotted the name, Dr. Simon Winter, on the note in the logbooks where the address was written. She would check on that later or have Brad check on it.

Back to the logbooks again. Josey hated loose ends. Because of the possible connection with the cigarette, she went back to the flights to San Salvador and reviewed the remarks over and over. "LP TKY023," she muttered aloud. "I can't think of anything else. That has to be a license plate, and 6 pax must refer to the number of passengers. He recorded those notes only on trips to San Salvador."

Trying not to let her overactive imagination get away from her, Josey envisioned a scenario involving illegal transportation of people or drugs. Seemed unbelievable. She couldn't imagine how Bobby thought he could get away with that sort of activity.

Her adrenaline was flowing, and when she got pumped up about an idea, Josey had a tendency to jump out on a limb and leave caution to the wind. She phoned Viscount special sales and asked about the next flight arriving from San Salvador.

"We have a flight arriving today at three thirty. It is showing on time. Gate twenty-six."

"Thanks. About how long does it take to get through customs?" Josey enquired.

"About an hour."

It was 2:45 in the afternoon. If she hurried,

Josey could be there when the flight from San Salvador arrived. She had to see who—or what—got off that plane. She wasn't sure what she'd do when she got there, but she couldn't sit at home wondering.

Josey lived only about fifteen minutes from the airport, so she grabbed her purse, her cell phone, and her digital camera and headed out.

Of course, when one is in a hurry, there is always an accident on the freeway. It looked like a small Toyota had collided with a Ford pickup as it was merging on to the freeway from the ramp. Even though the cars were off the road, the rubberneckers were still slowing down to check out the damage. That slowed Josey down, but she arrived at the airport a little after the flight touched down. What luck. She found a great place to park in the one-hour section of the parking garage directly across from the entrance that was closest to Gate twenty-six.

As she rushed across the crosswalk to the terminal building, she noticed a van parked in the loading area. It looked familiar. There was a handicap label hanging on the rearview mirror. A cardboard sign in the window was in Spanish. She wasn't sure what it meant—probably a destination or something. The only words she knew in Spanish were *señor* and *cerveza*—mister and beer!

Racking her brain for a connection, she finally remembered that she'd seen a van just like it at the clinic.

As Josey passed in front of the van, her eyes dropped to the license plate: TKY023. She almost hyperventilated as she gasped rapidly. Trying to get her bearings, she slowed down, hoping she hadn't been noticed. She thought, Oh, my God, what now? While Josey loved a good thriller, her tendency to take risks often led her to trouble. But now, faced with a scenario that could lead anywhere and even be dangerous, Josey had to step back and reconsider her actions.

It didn't take long for her to decide. She made a face and a gesture that she hoped would indicate that she had just remembered that she'd forgotten something. Then she turned and moved quickly back to her SUV. She settled in her seat and opened the windows to let in some air. She would see what—or who— entered the van.

Josey looked at the door to the van. There it was—the little medical symbol. She believed it was the same van she had seen at the clinic. Since the driver was nowhere in sight, she grabbed her digital camera, snapped a quick shot of the van, and put the camera into the armrest compartment of the car.

— ◆ —

Little did Josey know that the driver was the same man who had just invaded her home, Big Vern.

Along with his role as Murillo's bodyguard, Big Vern served many purposes at the clinic, including that of chauffeur. He had been blessed with an incredible memory for names and faces, but that was about it. He relied solely on his superiors when it came to decision making.

When Josey was walking by the van and noticing the license plate, Big Vern had been standing just inside the door waiting for his passengers to arrive. He spotted her looking at the van and thought she looked familiar. He tried to visualize where he might have seen her. His recollections were like dreams. It was almost as though he went into a trance when trying to remember. This time it popped up quickly. The vision of the woman became clear.

It was Josey Cantwell, the women whose house he had searched. He remembered seeing pictures of her in the office when he was searching for the documents. Vern watched with interest as she walked by the van and then made a quick about-face and hurried back to her car. He moved away from the airport entrance and pulled out his cell phone. "Boss, I think we have a problem here at the airport." He explained what he had observed. "What do you want me to do?"

Murillo gave Big Vern instructions.

"Do you have it with you?" Murillo asked.

Vern pulled the black nylon backpack off his shoulder and opened it. It contained a variety of items that he used in emergencies, and he rarely went anywhere without it. He looked inside and found a small kit.

"Yes, I have it. Don't worry. I'll take care of everything, just like you want," Big Vern told his boss—proud that he was always prepared. Then he went back into the terminal, walked past several exits, and proceeded to go back outside. He crossed the street and entered the parking garage.

As Josey watched and waited for something to happen with the van, she was startled as a large shadow darkened her window, cutting off the breeze. Before she could react, a needle was suddenly plunged into her arm. As she began to slump over in her seat, Big Vern opened the door and reached over her. He grabbed the keys from the ignition and pulled her purse from the unoccupied passenger seat. Before the drug took full effect, he carefully led her to the van as though she weighed nothing.

Josey looked up at Big Vern. She tried to cry for help, but no sound came out of her mouth. Big Vern's face was now burned into her memory, but then her vision blurred and she passed into a deep sleep.

Even as Josey fell limp, Vern had no problem giving the appearance that she was being assisted to the van of her own free will. He propped her upright in the back corner seat of the vehicle and arranged her so she appeared to be napping.

Just after he secured Josey's seatbelt, a group of three men and three women, all of Hispanic descent, arrived at the van. They were escorted by a young man in his early twenties.

— ✦ —

A skycap had noticed Vern putting Josey into the van, and he had noticed the arrival of the other passengers. He started to walk over to see if the lady was okay, but he quickly lost interest when a potential customer came into sight, dragging an assortment of heavy bags.

—◆—

With everyone settled in the van, Vern got into the driver's seat. He drove out of the terminal and headed toward the clinic.

Vern hadn't been expecting the extra passenger. He'd been forced to seat Maria, one of the three women, next to Josey. The young woman nudged Josey gently and, in broken English, asked, "You okay?" When Josey didn't respond, Maria asked the young escort if he knew what was wrong with the lady next to her. He just shrugged and told her not to worry—they were taking her to get some help.

Chapter 23

Cary got to Josey's house at about five that afternoon and found it empty. He looked around to see if his mother had left him a note and found nothing. He called Rene to see if she'd heard from their mother. "I'm sure she knew I was coming over tonight," he told his twin sister. "She said she was going to the store, but she should have been back by now. I can't believe she didn't at least leave a note. With all that's gone on recently, this is even more peculiar. Have you talked to her, Rene?"

"No. Why don't you call Brad? Maybe she went over to his house. You said she knew you were coming over."

"I thought she did. I told her that I was going to stay for a couple of nights. Look, I'm going to call Brad right away. I'll call you back."

Josey had Brad's number on speed dial at the house. Cary picked up the phone and dialed.

—◆—

Brad looked at the caller ID and saw the call was from Josey's phone. He picked up right away. "Josey," he said instead of the usual hello.

"No, it's Cary. I'm at Mom's, and she's not here. She's not at your place?"

"I haven't heard from her since we spoke earlier ... about two o'clock. I told her to stay put. But you know your mom. She never listens to anyone. She probably just ran to the store."

While Cary was talking to Brad, he was fumbling around with the bits and pieces of paper on Josey's desk. "I don't think so. I thought she'd have already finished up at the store by now. I guess she could have forgotten something and gone back. Maybe I'm just being paranoid. By the way, do you have any news about the break-in yet?"

Brad repeated the information he'd given to Josey earlier. "Nothing new since then. Have her call me as soon as she gets home."

—◆—

Cary had an uneasy feeling, but tried to push it aside. Sitting at his mother's desk, he picked up the plastic bag that held the cigarette inside and flipped it over and over in his hands. He wondered how the pieces fit together. His mother was really good at finding inconsistencies in her cases; and when she did, she had to determine why they existed. He only wished she could pick the predictable cases that were easy to resolve and unlikely to generate chaos in her life. But that wasn't her style.

Two hours passed, and Josey still hadn't returned. Cary tried calling her cell phone, but it went to voice mail. He left a message, but continued trying every ten minutes. He sent her a text. Still no response. He was really getting worried

Cary stared at his mother's desk as if it contained all the answers. It was a huge desk that took up one complete corner of her office. He remembered helping her move that monstrosity into the room. He'd told her that it was there for good because they would never get it out again.

Josey had scattered steno pads, legal pads, and small sticky note pads all over her desk. She had notes written on all of them. Her pattern was to grab the nearest note pad whenever she needed to jot something down. Then later she'd transcribe the notes to a variety of other notebooks organized by project. He didn't know how she found stuff and kept things organized. He wondered how Rene was able to do it.

His attention was drawn to the note sitting a little to the right of the PC monitor, just by the telephone. It looked like an airline schedule: "Viscount-3:30 pm, Gate 26." Cary subconsciously filed the information in the back of his mind and continued to peruse the paperwork on the desk. He really didn't know what he was looking for, but the activity helped keep him busy as he waited impatiently for his mother.

By eight o'clock that evening, Cary was beginning to panic. He called Rene and Brad again. Brad arrived in twenty minutes. The two of them were just about to try to make sense out of Josey's disappearance when Rene arrived.

"Rene, you should be home resting," Cary said, and Brad agreed heartily.

"Are you kidding? This involves me. I'm not leaving."

"I get it," said Cary. "And I don't want to freak you out, Rene, but something is wrong. I know it. First of all, Mom always calls us a couple of times a day. It can get a little annoying, but I just deal with it. You know how she is. Also, she hates to stay out late. She goes to bed early and gets up while it is still dark." He trusted his instincts. Like his mother's, they were typically right on.

"I agree, Cary," Rene said, her voice a bit shaky. "Brad, what are we going to do? I don't even know where to look. Should we call the police?"

"Not yet," said Brad. "Just be calm, darlin'. We are going to find her."

"You don't know our mom, Brad," Rene said. "Well, maybe you do, but even when she's on the road, she calls one of us. Cary even programmed her cell phone into the Bluetooth system in her car so she could go hands free when she's driving. She was a danger on the roads before that. And we got her a Bluetooth earpiece for when she's not in the car!" They were all aware of Josey's weird habits.

Cary wouldn't let it go. "With all that's going on, we would expect to hear from her every hour or so. But nothing—that's unusual. Something is wrong."

"Okay, kids. If she took off looking for something—which I wouldn't put past her— we need to see if we can track it down. Let's back up and see what we have so far—a cigarette, possible license plate number, some connection to San Salvador." Brad had dropped into his investigator mode; he had tuned out the twins.

"Wait, look at this!" Cary handed Brad the note with the Viscount flight number on it. "What do you think?"

Brad picked up the phone and called Viscount. The flight had arrived on time from San Salvador at 3:30 that same afternoon. "You know what I think? Your mom probably went to the airport to see what or who was on that flight. Cary, this may be futile, but why don't you and I run over to the airport? Maybe someone has seen her there." He turned to Rene. "Rene, you stay here at the house in case your mom calls. If anything happens, remember that Natasha is here. She can help."

Cary and Brad jumped into Brad's car and took off for the airport.

Just as they arrived in the departure area, they spotted a tow truck pulling up to a silver Mercedes SUV.

"My God, that's Mom's!"

Brad jerked the car to the right and almost landed on the sidewalk as he pulled to the curb. Cary jumped out and ran to the truck. The driver was just climbing down from the cab. "How long has this car been here?" Cary asked.

"I don't know. The police called us about two hours ago. This is the first chance we've had to pick it up. They usually check the license plate and try to contact the owner."

"I never got a call while I was at the house." Cary was frantic. "She couldn't have been in the terminal that long." He always carried a set of Josey's keys on his key chain as a backup in case she ever locked herself out of the car or house—something else she was prone to do. "Look," he said to the driver, "I have a set of keys here. This is my mom's car. I'll move it out of the way. Have you seen a police officer?"

"Yeah, the one who called this in is right inside the terminal."

Cary got in the car and immediately noticed Josey's cell phone sitting in the holder that was meant for drinks. He flung the door open and stepped outside. He yelled to Brad, who was just getting out of his car, having miraculously found a nearby parking space, and waved the phone back and forth in the air. "Brad! Her phone was still in the car. And the cop who called the tow truck is in the terminal."

"Just go park the car and meet me inside," Brad yelled as he jogged toward the terminal entrance.

While Cary moved the car, Brad ran inside to find the police officer. Josey was missing. A familiar chill went up Brad's spine. Here we go again, he thought. Why can't she just stay put for a change and ask me for help? He could feel his heart beating triple time. The thought that something might have happened to Josey hit him like a brick.

Brad spotted an officer just a few yards away. As he explained the situation, the policeman started taking down all the information.

—◆—

A missing person at DFW airport was something the officer didn't want to deal with. It would definitely draw in media attention. He could taste his lunch surging back up his throat just thinking about it.

The skycap who had been watching Big Vern earlier as he put Josey into the van walked over to see what was going on. "What's up?" he asked as he approached Brad and the police officer.

The police officer didn't respond, but Brad told him what was going on. When he heard the problem, the skycap stood at attention. "I didn't think nothin' of it at the time, but I did see a big fellow—really big—helping a lady out of the Mercedes and putting her in a van. Didn't look suspicious at the time. She looked tired or like she didn't feel too good. I never gave it much thought after that because things got busy, and I left to help some passengers with their luggage. Now that I think about it though, she could have been drugged up. The guy was so big, it didn't seem like it was any effort at all for him to put her in the van."

"Can you give us more of a description?" the policeman asked.

"Let me think ..." The mercenary skycap stonewalled.

"Will this help you think faster?" Brad asked as he pulled out a wad of bills, peeled several off, and waved them in front of the skycap.

The skycap's eyes opened wide, and he held out his hand, into which Brad slammed a few bills. "Yeah, like I said, a big fellow. Odd looking for an old guy. He had long gray hair in a ponytail." He put the bills into his pocket.

"Do you remember what the van looked like? How big was it? Ten passengers? Twenty? What color was it? Did you see the license number?" Brad spouted out more questions.

"Slow down, dude. Let me think. I never pay much attention to those things. There's billions of vans come in and out this place." After a pause he said, "I think I remember seeing a bunch of Spanish-looking people getting in the van. Maybe five or six total."

—◆—

After moving the car, while Brad talked to the police officer and the skycap, Cary had run into the terminal building and started asking the agents if anyone remembered seeing Josey. The sentimental type, Cary pulled out his wallet and displayed a picture of Josey and her grandkids to the agents and skycaps.

Feeling frustrated, Cary saw Brad and the policeman talking to the skycap and ran over to them. "I can't find out anything." The strain in his voice was evident.

—◆—

"We may have some clues." Brad tried to be calm, but he could feel his blood pressure rising. "The police are going to fingerprint the car. It has to be the same person that broke into Josey's house. We'll have the fingerprints compared to those on the cigarette. I'll see if the police can put out an APB on a van that matches the description from the skycap. It's a longshot, but we need to try everything."

"I'll call Rene," Cary said, his voice shaking, "and have her start combing through Mom's desk again to see if anything might make sense.

"It will be okay, Cary." Brad tried to calm him down, all the time he was just as worried.

Chapter 24

Josey felt sluggish from the drugs when she woke up, but not sluggish enough to keep her from feeling a sense of panic when she found herself in what looked like a doctor's examining room. She was freezing as she lay on a standard white examination table.

She sat up and looked at her naked arm trying to focus on a watch that wasn't there. She felt her neck and was glad she hadn't put her necklace on that morning. She wondered where she was and how long she'd been unconscious. They had taken her clothes, and she was wearing a white hospital gown sporting little pink squares. She felt around the garment for a hole in the back. Darn, it was open all the way down the back—just a tie at the top. At least they hadn't taken her underwear. She looked around for her clothes, but they were nowhere in sight.

She slid off the table and walked around the room trying to shake off the remnants of the drug that had knocked her out. A lone chair and a stool with casters on the legs were the only other pieces of furniture in the room. There were no pictures or posters on the walls, only a mirror that looked about twenty-four inches square. She wondered if it was a one-way mirror. The room was sterile looking; absolutely everything was white. There was a counter with cabinets above and drawers below, but the counter was totally void of the usual tongue depressors and other medical supplies that one typically saw in an examining room.

"Wait a minute," she said out loud. She began to figure out where she was. They had taken her back to the clinic. That was the only place she could be, considering she was in an examination room. What she couldn't figure out was why. What could she know that would cause someone to do this to her?

She made her way to the door. It was locked— of course. Whoever had abducted her certainly wasn't going to make it easy for her to leave.

Concentrating now, trying to focus, Josey began to explore. While awkwardly trying to hold the back of her gown together, she opened the cabinets and drawers—all empty. She stared into the mirror. It was built into the wall, but she couldn't tell if it really was the kind that someone could see through from one side but not the other. There were no windows. She lowered herself into the chair. Now what? She was getting claustrophobic.

Josey heard a door close. It seemed to come from the room next to hers. She heard muffled voices.

—◆—

Allemand and Murillo watched her from the adjoining room through the one-way mirror.

"It's her all right. The one working on the Cisco case," Allemand said, recalling the picture he had seen of her on the book in Tony's office. "Why did you have to take her? Wasn't there any other way to deal with this? What do you plan to do with her?" he asked, clearly fearing the worst. Although awash in criminal activity himself, he didn't want to be involved in deciding how to deal with Josey Cantwell.

Murillo said, "We know she was here earlier today asking questions. We caught her image on the security videotapes. The security guard had the pictures sitting on his desk, and of course Vern recognized her from his surveillance of her house. First we need to see if we can find out how much she knows and who else might have any information." This issue had suddenly moved forward on Murillo's list of priorities. He was glad he had already arrived in Dallas by the time this had happened.

"How hard do you think it will be to get her to talk?" Allemand asked. "I don't want her to see me. What if something happens and she can identify me? I won't have it."

"She won't see either one of us. The doctors here have the means. They'll get what we need, and then we'll take care of her. Just like the others," Murillo said as he sized up the situation.

"Let's find out what she knows," Allemand said.

—✦—

"I guess I really did it this time," Josey concluded as she sat back on the edge of the examination table. All she could do was wait and pray—and pray some more. Brad and Cary were right. I do get myself into these messes. I just hope they can figure out where I am and get me out.

Even though Josey worked hard to stay calm, her fear intensified. She started experiencing chest pains—symptoms not unusual for her when her stress level rose. She knew it was stress and that it was merely esophageal spasms. It had happened before, and she had learned how to deal with it by simply relaxing and breathing slowly. The pains always went away. All she had to work with now was her mind and her uncanny ability to solve puzzles.

Her only hope was to stall her captors for as long as possible. She knew that, when Brad discovered she was missing, he wouldn't rest until he found her.

Maybe she could make this pain in her chest work to her advantage. Josey deliberately started to hyperventilate. She grabbed her chest. She fell over in her chair and dropped to the floor.

—◆—

Dr. Winter, a tall, gangly black man with bushy eyebrows and short curly hair, ran into the room followed by the nurse on duty. Together, they lifted Josey back onto the table, and the nurse checked her blood pressure. "Her blood pressure is one eighty-nine over ninety.

"We need to get her settled down," said Dr. Winter. "I'd say this is stress related." He walked out of the room and approached Allemand and Murillo. "Was she drugged? What is going on here? Who is this woman?"

"Don't you worry about it. Just do your job," Murillo said with authority.

The doctor backed off and returned to the room.

—◆—

Josey could tell that her face was bright red. She started to perspire, and her hands were all clammy. While she really knew she was going to be okay, she was still nervous—her chest actually was hurting. "My chest ... I can't breathe ... my arm feels funny." Josey could have won an academy award for that scene. She recognized the nurse as the woman who had come into the reception area while she was investigating the clinic. This confirmed her suspicion as to her location.

"Quick, let's get an EKG," Dr. Winter said to the nurse, who rushed out of the room. To Josey he said, "Just be calm." The nurse quickly returned with the EKG machine on a rolling cart. Josey soon felt the goop being applied to her chest and legs as the nurse and the doctor worked together to attach the leads to her body. She could see the lines forming on the paper as the thin marker slid gently back and forth, making an occasional jig when it should have jagged. She watched the doctor's face as he monitored the readings. "There is an abnormality on this reading. We need to take more tests." Suddenly, he raised his voice, "Quick, get a nitro pill," he ordered.

The nurse quickly produced a little white pill from somewhere on the cart and stuck it under Josey's tongue.

"We need to find out what she knows. After that, I couldn't care less," said the doctor.

The doctor had no way of knowing that the "abnormal" EKG reading was normal for Josey. Because of this odd reading, she'd been forced to endure a few nuclear stress EKGs in the past, and they had all came out normal.

—✦—

"Now look!" Allemand cried to Murillo. "She's so scared she's having a heart attack!" He stared into the one-way mirror.

"That certainly would make things easier," Murillo said coldly.

"We need to know if anyone else is aware of what we're doing. My whole future is at stake here. We can't let her die now." Allemand started pacing.

As the two men stared at Josey, the doctor entered the outer room and spoke to them. "I don't believe she's had a heart attack. She's stable now, and she needs to rest. Look, I'm in this as deep as you are, but we can't let these undocumented people be linked to us.

Killing a US citizen—especially one who has the visibility this woman has—is above my pay grade."

"We need the information," said Allemand.

The doctor raised his hands, directing Allemand to back off. "If you try to interrogate her now, you might aggravate her condition, and you won't find out anything. Let me take a look at her in the morning and I'll let you know then."

—✦—

The doctor was also starting to have second thoughts about this. He was making a bundle here. His wife lived in luxury, and his kids went to the finest schools. How could he have been so stupid as to allow himself to get involved?

—✦—

"But..." Allemand was in a panic.

Murillo pulled at Allemand's arm. "The doctor said she needs rest. Let her rest. She isn't going anywhere. In the meantime, I'll have Big Vern get back over to her house and see if he can find anything now." Murillo was accustomed to dealing with difficult situations. They were no big deal to him.

Murillo turned to Dr. Winter. "Look here, Doctor, you aren't going to escape this now. It won't take long for the AMA and police to find out about your drug problem and the boy you accidentally killed while under the influence. We saved your butt, and you are not going to screw this up." Murillo's tone was smooth, but lethal.

The doctor nodded. "In the morning. I'll do it then." He walked away.

Allemand, on the other hand, was on the verge of having his own heart attack.

Chapter 25

Cary drove Josey's SUV back to her house and arrived just after Brad had pulled into the driveway. It was getting late, but there was no rest in sight until they found Josey.

Rene was still there. Tears started rolling down her cheeks as soon as she saw her brother.

"Did you find her? What is going on?" She knew she had to get herself together if she was going to be any help at all.

"Where's Adam?" Cary asked.

"He's at home with Matt."

"You should be there too."

"Like that's going to happen. I'm not leaving until we find Mom," Rene insisted.

—◆—

Cary and Rene knew about Brad's CIA background, but they had never seen him in action until now. Brad was on the phone calling in all his chips from his buddies at the agency. Josey and her family were the most important people in his life, and he couldn't accept the thought of losing her. He needed to stay calm and fall back on his instincts and years of training and experience.

While Brad was working his end, the kids were back in Josey's office sorting through the case files to see if they could come up with any more useful information.

Finally, Brad came into Josey's office. "Well, I found out one thing so far," Brad said. "The fingerprints on the car are the same as those on the cigarette. They're trying to run them down, but so far can't find a match. My guess is that they belong to someone from El Salvador, and it may be hard to pin him down. But we know there's a link." He sat down hard on Josey's chair. "Okay, let's go over this again." Brad visualized a list in his head. "Josey followed a lead that directed her to a Viscount flight arrival. Some big guy led Josey and another five or six passengers into the van.

"M—maybe this is something," Rene stammered as she picked up the piece of paper that identified the Dallas address. "Look, here ... this came from the Cisco documents, but see here ... she made a copy of it." She pointed to the duplicate of the address that had been tossed to the side of the other papers. "I wonder how we missed this."

"We don't have much else. Let's check it out," Brad said as he gave her a reassuring hug. "Rene, you stay here while Cary and I go take a look. Lock all three bolts and stay inside. I mean it! You have my cell phone number if you need to talk to me. If anything makes you nervous, get Natasha. She'll keep you company, and she's stronger and more capable than she looks."

"We'll take my car," Brad said as he ran to his Mercedes, which was parked in the driveway. Cary was close on his heels. Brad was already packing a gun, but as soon as he settled himself in the driver's seat, he reached over and pulled out two additional guns from the glove compartment. He checked to be sure they were loaded. He handed one to Cary and tucked the other one next to the console between the seats. "Ever use a gun before?" Brad asked Cary.

"In the guard," Cary said as he took the gun and laid it down next to him. "Just practice. Do you really think we'll need guns? The thought of actually using a gun makes me uneasy."

"Well, considering what has already happened

to Rene, we need to be prepared for anything. The guns are just a precaution. Haven't used this in a while myself." He patted his holster. "Let's hope we won't have to now."

"What do you mean 'in a while'?" Cary looked at Brad.

Cary waited for a response.

Brad didn't respond.

It was well past midnight as Cary and Brad took off in search of Josey.

Chapter 26

Back at the clinic, Dr. Winter checked on Josey. He left her room and told the nurse to give her a mild sedative to calm her down. He was pulling an all-nighter, but there was a comfortable room for the doctors on duty, so he headed that way.

—◆—

"Here, take this," the nurse said as she handed Josey a pill with a glass of water.

Josey was surprised, but glad, that they hadn't given her another shot. She put the pill in her mouth and sipped the water, but she didn't swallow the pill. It was fortunate the nurse left right away. Josey was afraid the nurse would wait to be sure she took the pill, but she took off without noticing. Josey spit out what was left of the pill and held it between her fingers until she could find a place to drop it. She hoped that the amount she did ingest wouldn't render her useless.

She was still groggy, and her head was starting to hurt from the nitro pill. They had moved her to another room. This one had a window, but it was, again, sparsely furnished. She hadn't realized how much color played a part in her life until she'd been imprisoned in those white, sterile surroundings. At least there wasn't anything that could be a two-way mirror.

Josey pulled the covers up to her neck and closed her eyes.

The doctor came in for one last look. "Where is the nurse?" He looked around. "Oh well, you're not going anywhere for a while. I'll check on you in the morning." He walked out, shutting the door behind him.

The partial pill was having some effect. Josey was tired, but believed she could force herself to stay alert. Maybe the medicine would at least help get rid of the pounding headache.

Josey managed to get up and go over to the window. It was barred. No surprise there. The full moon lit up the landscape like a huge spotlight in the sky. Out of habit, she looked at her arm to check the time. She had forgotten—her watch was gone. It had to be late. So much had happened that day.

She was tired and woozy, but the sedative's impact did help reduce her anxiety. She had to muster up the strength to find a way out. She couldn't stay there waiting for them to come back in the morning. Her sixth sense was telling her that the likelihood of getting out of this place in one piece wasn't good.

Josey reached around to the open back of her hospital gown. She could feel the cool air from the ventilation system blowing on her exposed back and bottom. As she looked around the room, she spotted another gown folded on the counter. She put it on over the other gown with the opening in the front—problem solved.

She thought of the twenty-third psalm. "Though I walk through the valley of the shadow of death," she whispered, "You are with me. Please be with me, Lord."

Still dressed in the hospital attire and barefoot, Josey was resolved to get out of there. She instinctively went to the door and turned the handle. "Thank you, Lord!" she exclaimed to herself. It was unlocked—a blessing. Carefully, she peeked outside and saw that the hallway was clear.

The clinic looked deserted. Unlike other clinics and hospitals she'd been in, this one didn't have nurses' stations or waiting areas out in the open. The place reminded her more of a hotel. Everything appeared to be isolated in rooms or offices. She wasn't sure which way to go, and she definitely didn't want to walk into the wrong room. She was careful not to retrace the path that led to this room.

She didn't see any exit signs. Some of the doors had identification plates and some didn't.

She forgot to breathe again. She told herself to calm down. Just take slow, deep breaths and keep going. She figured it couldn't get any worse. This was her only chance for escape.

Josey opened a double door with no identification plate. She peeked inside and saw what looked like a hospital ward. A quick glance revealed about ten beds, all occupied. The occupants were asleep. That was peculiar. For a clinic as plush as this appeared to be, why would they put people in a ward instead of private rooms?

She was careful not to make a sound as she closed the door and continued down the hall. As she passed another room, she overheard the voices of two men. She paused with her back to the wall and listened.

"Don't worry, we'll get rid of her," one man said.

"Isn't there another way?" replied another man.

She could hear one of them pacing the floor. A step, thud, step, thud—he was limping!

Josey didn't need to wait around to hear more. She knew what they were discussing—her demise! She took another deep breath and cautiously moved on, anxious to get away before they discovered her disappearance.

Her body trembled with fear and from the chilled air that filtered through the hallway. Suddenly, she heard a door handle turning.

Josey froze momentarily in her tracks. She saw the plate on the door next to her. It was marked "Lab." She had no choice but to duck in. She was thankful it was the middle of the night. No one was working.

The room was dimly lit by a couple of night-lights near the worktables. It was even colder in the lab. The lighting was barely bright enough to keep an employee from tripping over something. As Josey walked around the lab looking for another exit, she noticed a large door with a window about one foot square cut into it. The interior was dimly lit. She couldn't resist the temptation to take a quick glance inside. She had to stretch on her toes to get a good look.

It was a freezer. Inside were three stainless steel tables about six feet long, waist high, and positioned in a row. On each surface lay a body. Hanging from each body was a toe tag. She could read two of the labels: "Pax 1" and "Pax 2." The passengers from El Salvador! There was no question about it. They were dead!

Oh, my God! I have got to get out of here. What a nightmare! Would she end up like those guys in the freezer, another hard body on a cold slab with a toe tag—perhaps "Pax 4"?

As she lowered her heels back to the floor, an eerie feeling of warmth permeated the skin on her back in the otherwise frigid room. Afraid to turn, she took a deep breath and held it. She stood frozen as a rigid hand touched her shoulder. She opened her mouth in fear, but nothing came out.

"Help me," came a soft cry from behind her.

Carefully turning so as not to create a scene, Josey found herself staring at a young— maybe nineteen- or twenty-year-old—stout girl of Hispanic descent. The young girl's eyes were pleading. "Por favor. Help me," she whispered again as tears streamed down her face.

"Who ...?" Josey started to say, but was quickly brought back to reality. There was no time to figure it out now. "Go back," she gestured.

"Please, take me away from here," the girl pleaded.

Josey sighed. It was a sigh of relief that she hadn't been caught, a sigh of determination to escape, and a sigh of concern about what to do with the girl.

With wobbly knees and a heart that was racing again, Josey looked around until she spotted another door. Again, she slowly peeked through the opening. It led to another hallway. She had to take her chances. Peering down the hallway, she finally saw it. It was an exit.

She grabbed the girl by the arm and put her finger to her mouth indicating silence. Together they headed through the door and down the hallway.

The exit door was the kind that could be opened from the inside, but was locked from the outside. Josey pushed the door open and hesitated to see if an alarm would go off. Nothing. Relief.

The two women stepped out of the building and gently shut the door behind them. Standing still next to the door, they waited another moment as they heard voices around the corner in the parking lot. Josey pulled the girl down with her behind a bush. They huddled as close to the ground as possible, their backs flush against the building, holding their breath in spine-chilling silence.

The night was still, and the voices were clear. They sounded like the men Josey had overheard in the office. They made no attempt to keep their voices low. The women heard every word.

"I don't care how you get the information, just do it and let me know as soon as possible," one of the men said with fear in his voice. Again Josey heard the step, thud, step thud of the unknown man with the limp, this time on the gravelly tarmac.

Josey heard a car door shut and the sound of an automobile driving away. She waited to see if another door shut, but heard nothing. The other man must still be there. She knew they couldn't wait any longer. She had to get away from there and hoped the young woman had the stamina and courage to continue their journey to freedom.

Josey looked for an escape route away from the building and found that they were trapped within a security fence. The young girl was relying on Josey to lead her. Although Josey was frightened, the added responsibility of another person's survival heightened her resolve and courage.

Now what? Josey directed her refugee with as much stealth as she could muster up. They made their way around the building, staying close to the wall until she spotted a gate used for deliveries. It didn't go all the way to the ground. Leaving the young girl at the wall, she sprinted across to the short expanse to the gate and lay flat, with her stomach on the ground. Carefully she eased her way underneath the gate, barely making it. Despite the several abrasions from the uneven and rocky driveway beneath her, she motioned for the young girl to hurry and scoot under the fence. The young girl obeyed and struggled to squeeze through, but made it.

Josey managed a weak smile and said, "We should be safe now. I don't see anyone coming. Let's get out of here."

—✦—

Josey had been wrong. There was an alarm, only she hadn't heard it. Inside the building, the drowsy security guard was brought to his feet when a steady beep penetrated the room. He stood, alert, looking at the array of monitors, quickly moving from screen to screen until he saw Murillo standing in the parking lot next to his car. His boss must have accidentally triggered the alarm without thinking. The security guard relaxed, got up, and tucked in his shirt. He looked around for his hat. He didn't want Murillo to think he was a slob.

Not seeing anything out of order, he turned away from the monitors to check outside. Just as he got up and turned around, the picture on one of the security monitors rotated around to expose the two women moving toward the gate—an oversight the guard would later regret.

Expending little energy, the guard sauntered outside to the parking lot as he tried to figure out how to diplomatically tell his boss about the nighttime security procedure. He smiled thinking that he'd be praised for being so alert.

Murillo looked around as he heard the guard exit the building and walk toward him. "What's the problem?" he said.

"No problem, really, sir," the guard said, standing at ease. "Sir, sorry to bother you, but the security alarm just went off. I just want to be sure you know that you need to use your security card when you leave the building at night."

"I did use my card," Murillo said. "There must be something wrong with the alarm."

"No, sir, I don't think so."

Murillo stopped. Then it hit him. "No, she couldn't have gotten away. She was drugged!"

"Who, sir?"

"The Cantwell woman!" Murillo said. Go check around the building just in case," Murillo roared as he sprinted back into the building as fast as he could to check on Josey.

Since he wasn't sure where they had put Josey, he went directly to the night nurse who was resting in an easy chair in the nurses' lounge.

"Where is she? Where did you put that Cantwell woman?" he asked as he grabbed the nurse by the arm, pinching her so hard she shrieked from the pain. She tried to get away, but he kept holding on as he pulled her outside the lounge.

"Over there," the nurse said as she pointed to Josey's room.

Murillo pulled the door open. Empty. He turned and started running toward the exit again.

"She's gone! Quick! Come with me! We have to find her."

Josey and the girl were so far away they barely heard the loud voices of the men. Josey's instincts told her to keep running, and she pulled on the girl's arm as they ran like hell. Too fast, in fact, because Josey stumbled over her own feet and instantly hit the pavement. The girl bumped into Josey, and they landed in a pile.

Josey withheld the urge to scream when she hit her knee against a sharp rock, causing a nasty gash. The palms of her hands were skinned from bracing herself against the fall. Not even looking down at her knee to assess the damage, she jumped back up, grabbed the girl's hand, and resumed running.

They heard the men yelling orders at each other.

— ✦ —

"She can't be too far," Murillo said. "Get some help. Let's find her!"

The guard took off immediately, not having a clue what direction to go in. The area around the clinic was a jumble of open spaces, parking lots, and locked buildings. There was a low-income housing development nearby— more places to hide. He headed that way.

Josey had to find a place to hide so they could catch their breath. They ran through the back streets until she spotted an old run-down convenience store located in the middle of a seedy housing development. She couldn't tell if it was just closed for the night or out of business. She moved quickly around the building until she spotted the doors to the restrooms. "Come on," Josey directed the girl.

The girl nodded, her eyes still bulging with fear and her face bright red from the chase.

Josey tried to open the ladies' room door. She turned the knob and pushed hard. It was locked. She tried the men's room. The door was jammed, but she tugged harder, and it finally opened. She pulled the girl inside, pushed the door until it closed, and turned the latch on the doorknob to lock it.

She didn't try to find the light switch, fearful it would give them away. It was better that she didn't know what was in there anyway. The stench was overpowering, and the floor under her bleeding bare feet was sticky—almost gooey, as if the room hadn't been cleaned for years. The two of them clung tightly to each other and tried not to move around, afraid to touch anything.

Josey gagged and tried hard not to vomit. She prayed the young girl wouldn't panic and would stay quiet.

Suddenly Josey felt something crawl up onto her bare foot. She lifted her foot and tried to shake it off. She started to think she might be better off surrendering than to stay in this public restroom from hell any longer. What had possessed her to pick a place like this?

Then she heard a noise. Footsteps outside. She stood still, the creature still clinging to her foot and beginning to make its way up her leg while the young girl hung tightly to her side, shaking silently in the darkness.

—◆—

The guard was running aimlessly through the neighborhood when he heard dogs barking. He stopped to determine the direction of the noise and concluded that there wasn't much else to bark at this time of night except maybe someone intruding on their territory.

As he continued his trek, he caught a glimpse of the convenience store on his right. He listened for the dogs—the barking had subsided.

He walked slowly around the building shining his flashlight into the windows and jiggling the knobs to the doors. As he walked to the side of the building he spotted the ladies' room and tried to turn the knob. It was locked. Those doors were often unlocked, and this would be a good place to hide, he thought. If she was in there, he'd get her. He pulled out his gun and aimed it at the doorknob.

—◆—

The sound of the gun blast pierced Josey's ears. She forgot all about the bug—or worse—and started praying again. The young girl was still shaking violently at her side.

They heard the guard push the decimated women's door in. They knew he wouldn't find anything there. Then they heard his footsteps resound as he approached their hideout. Josey froze as she heard the doorknob jiggle. He was going to kill them. This was it. They were going to die.

The dogs started barking again. The jiggling stopped. The guard spoke. "They must have gone that way." They heard him go off in the direction of the noise, the sound of his clomping footsteps dissipating as he ran down the street.

Still standing stiff as a board, Josey waited for what seemed an eternity with her ears tuned to the outside. Then she finally let out a breath and tried to gain her composure. The bug was still crawling on her leg. She shook herself vigorously, and it finally let go.

"Thank you," Josey said as she peered up into the darkness. "You spared me again."

She couldn't stay in that cesspool a minute longer, so she slowly opened the door and peeked outside. The night was still. The air was fresh.

The young girl was clenching Josey's arm as they walked out of the building.

"Come on," Josey whispered. She loosened the girl's hand from her arm and motioned her to follow. With extreme caution, they moved away from the building and worked their way farther into the run-down housing area. They soon picked up the pace and continued running as fast as they could considering the injuries both had incurred and that they were barefoot.

Josey's leg was starting to throb. Her knee. She finally looked down at it. In the moonlight she could see that she had a nasty cut. It was still bleeding.

"You bleeding! You hurt!" the girl said in broken English.

"I'm okay," Josey replied softly, again putting her finger to her mouth indicating quiet.

She didn't think it was too serious, but she needed to tend to it. She tore the sleeve out of the arm of the hospital gown and tied it around her leg to keep it straight and hopefully hold back the blood flow.

A thick cloud cover drifted across the once-bright moon, darkening the sky and making it harder for Josey to see where they were going. While the darkness made her more frightened, she knew that it would also make it harder for her adversaries to find them.

Josey's breathing became labored. She glanced at the girl, who was also gasping for breath. She slowed down to a brisk pace until they came upon an old strip shopping center with a small grocery store, a dollar store, and a self-service laundry. Josey's feet were killing her; they were torn up from the rough ground. This wasn't the best part of town, but after what she'd just been through, she didn't care.

"Look, there's a payphone!" A phone was attached to the outside wall at the end of the building. "Sit here." Josey pointed to the ground next to the phone. "Rest."

The girl obeyed without comment.

"Please work, please work ..." Josey picked up the receiver and hit the "0" to get an operator.

"Operator." The voice on the other ear came through loud and clear.

It worked. "Thank God." With the luck she'd been having, she was sure the phone would be out of order—like most of the phones she tried in the past. "I want to place a collect call to 555-521-0240."

— ◆ —

Rene jumped when the phone rang. She immediately accepted the charges. "Mom, oh, Mom, are you okay? Where are you? We're crazy here! We found a note in your office with a Dallas address on it. Brad and Cary are headed that way."

"Good sleuthing," Josey said, the words barely audible. "They shouldn't be too far from here."

"Mom ..."

"I'm okay. Well, not totally okay ... but safe for now. I'll tell you later. This place is spooky. Tell them to hurry." Josey tried to console Rene who was weeping on the other line.

Josey let the phone hang on the cord while

she ran to the corner to see the street names more clearly. She ran back and repeated the street names to Rene. She knew Brad wouldn't have any problem finding her.

Josey replaced the receiver gently and gratefully. She looked down at the girl who was finally breathing normally and held out her hand. The girl reached up, and Josey pulled her to her feet. They walked around to the side of the building, and Josey found a place to sit out of sight of the road while she waited for Brad and Cary to arrive. She took a few deep breaths in an attempt to lessen her anxiety. It didn't work.

Josey looked at the frightened girl and then down at her own torn hospital gown and battered legs. What a sight, she thought.

"What's your name?" she finally asked the young girl. It felt odd not knowing the name of the person with whom she'd just shared a life-threatening experience.

"Maria," the young girl answered.

"I'm Josey."

"Thank you, Miss Josey," Maria continued.

"We'll be okay now. Help is on the way," Josey reassured her.

"Thank you for saving me." Maria began to weep again.

Josey nodded to the girl. The adrenaline boost she'd managed to muster for their escape was starting to decline, and she began to have trouble holding her head up.

Maria sat in silence.

—◆—

When Brad got Rene's call, they were almost at the clinic. Relief spread through his tense muscles. He looked over at Cary. "Josey just called Rene from a pay phone. We're close. She's at a strip mall down the street from here."

Brad's vintage car was equipped with a non-vintage GPS. He punched in the street names and a vivid map instantly popped up delineating the route. A mechanical-sounding female voice began to speak out directions, "In two hundred feet, turn right."

Brad stepped on the gas.

"How is she?" Cary asked.

"Rene said she didn't sound too good."

In no time, they located the shopping center. Brad pulled in and got out of the car as fast as he could, Cary right behind him. "Where is she?" Brad cried out when they didn't see her right away. He ran around to the side of the building. "Oh, my God," Brad exclaimed when he saw Josey slumped over on the ground almost invisible in the shadows of the building. "Josey!" His voice was low and gentle. He leaned over her and touched her shoulder trying not to startle her.

Josey, still dazed by the events, hadn't heard the car. She jumped, frightened out of her wits until she realized it was Brad. Maria, not knowing Brad, remained huddled close to Josey.

"Oh, Brad, I'm so glad to see you." She tried to get up. "It was a nightmare. They drugged me and took me to their clinic."

"Shhh. Not now. Let's get out of here."

Both men stopped when they realized Josey wasn't alone. They stared at Maria.

"Who is this?" Brad asked, sounding confused, as he ran his fingers through his thick hair.

"This is Maria," Josey answered, gesturing with her hand.

She looked at Maria and back to Brad. "Maria, it's okay. They are friends."

"Just stay quiet for now. We'll talk later," Brad said as he lifted Josey off the ground with a gentleness most never saw, and carried her to the car.

Cary stared at his mother, holding back a tear as he saw her blood-stained clothing and the wounds on her legs and feet. "Should we take her to the hospital?" he asked Brad.

"No. Looks like just minor cuts and scratches. She'll be okay once she's cleaned up. What she really needs is rest," Brad said as he positioned her in the back seat of the car.

Cary helped Maria up and escorted her to the car.

Josey looked over at Maria, who was staring at her.

"It's okay, Maria. We'll help you." Josey smiled. Relieved to be safely harnessed in Brad's familiar car, she immediately drifted off to sleep, not even trying to fight to stay awake.

Chapter 27

The guards who had gone out on foot looking for Josey returned empty handed.

"How could you let this happen?" Murillo raised his voice. He tried to be smooth, but his clenched fists gave him away.

One of the guards stepped forward. "She had a good start on us. She could be anywhere by now." Murillo knew the guard was fearful for his job and maybe even his life.

"She can't be far. Get in your car and keep searching the area," Murillo ordered. "Quick, you"—he pointed to the nurse who had run outside with him—"continue searching the building. We have to find her. Maybe she's hiding in there." As she turned to run, Murillo grabbed her by the arm and spun her around. "Why didn't someone check on her during the night?" he demanded. "Which doctor is on duty?"

"Dr. Winter." The nurse was rubbing her arm, where Murillo had left bruises from pinching her so hard.

"Get him. Now!"

The nurse took off.

The staff was in a panic. Murillo was certain they didn't want his wrath to fall on them. He turned back to see the guard still standing there. "What are you waiting for?" he screamed.

"We covered every nook and cranny within a three mile radius. It's dark. She could have hidden anywhere or somehow hitched a ride. There's no sense spinning our wheels on this any longer. The area is too vast to cover." The guard backed away slowly as he spoke.

—◆—

Dr. Winter staggered down the hall, the nurse behind him. He was still drowsy from being awoken. As Murillo approached, he started to speak, "What is—"

Murillo stood there, flanked by the two guards. He was livid. He didn't let Dr. Winter finish. "How could you let that Cantwell woman just slip out of the clinic? Incompetents!"

"We didn't expect this to happen. She was drugged. I don't know how she slipped out," the doctor replied.

"Where's Big Vern?" Murillo asked to anyone who might have an answer.

"Don't you remember?" the nurse replied. "Big Vern isn't here. You sent him off somewhere."

Murillo recalled that he had sent Big Vern back to Josey's house. He immediately picked up the phone and placed a call. "Where are you, Vern?"

Vern answered on the first ring. "I'm outside the house. Her daughter is in there, and I was going to wait until she left before I went in."

"Well, we have problems. That Cantwell woman got away. She's probably on her way home now. Here is what I want you to do." Murillo gave specific instructions. His typical calm demeanor was starting to erode.

"No problem, boss."

— ◆ —

Big Vern had driven the clinic van again. He opened the back of the van and pulled out some rope. He stuffed it into a medium-size pack, which he then secured around his waist. He got back into the driver's seat and eased the van a bit farther down the road, not wanting to draw attention to the vehicle, especially as he'd used the same one during his previous break-in. Silently, he got out of the van, removed his gun from his holster, and moved to the gate that led to the backyard of Josey's house. He was surprised to find that it was locked this time. Not wanting to be seen jumping the fence, he moved around to the back of the yard. This part of the property was bordered by a vacant lot, and he knew he wouldn't be seen climbing over the fence.

Vern moved along the shadow of the house to the master bedroom. He took care to be quiet as he jimmied the door and went inside. There wasn't much time. He remembered the floor plan from his other visit.

As he entered the hallway, he found Rene in the living room on the couch. She was awake, but she looked as if she was just about to doze off.

Big Vern moved over behind couch. He leaned in and put his hand over her mouth.

Paralyzed with fear, Rene couldn't move at all. She stared at the gun pointed at her.

"I see we meet again." Vern's mouth twisted up into a grin and then just as quickly turned down into a menacing sneer. "This time you're coming with me. Keep quiet."

Vern took his hand off her mouth. Rene tried to speak, but nothing would come out.

"Don't yell or I'll use this," Vern emphasized as he pointed the gun to her head. "Stay still."

Vern took the rope out of his pack and tied Rene's hands in front of her. Then he pulled her up off the couch.

Rene cringed as the ropes rubbed against her skin.

Still pointing the gun at her, Vern pushed her along into Josey's office.

The logbook copies were sitting in the middle of the desk. Vern spotted them right away. He grabbed the documents and stuffed them into his pack.

Rene began to struggle under his grip. Vern was surprised at her feistiness, but he held her tight. He laughed at her feeble attempts to free herself.

Rene's legs buckled. Vern yanked her up and dragged her toward the door. "Move!" He wagged the gun in front of her face. "You're coming with me."

—◆—

Brad and Cary sat in silence as they drove back to Josey's house, each in his own thoughts.

They were both relieved to have Josey back, but they were plotting separately how they would get even with the people who had done this to her. Each was wondering who Maria was and what part she had played in this conspiracy.

They didn't want to disturb Josey, who was dozing in the backseat. Brad could hear her soft snoring.

Just as they were approaching Josey's house, Brad spotted a large man who was busy dragging someone toward a van.

"Hey, what's going on here? What's this?" Brad exclaimed so loud that it jolted Josey from her sleep. She lifted her head above the seat to see what he was talking about.

"That's the van, Brad! The one from the clinic!" Josey screamed as she pointed to the vehicle. "He has Rene!"

Brad threw his arm back and motioned for Josey to lie back down. Still weak, she complied. "Stay down, Josey. We'll take care of this."

Maria cowered in the corner of the car seat.

Instinctively, almost before he could put the car in park, Brad was out of the car, gun in hand, running toward the van. Without a word, Cary grabbed the other gun, jumped out, and followed him.

—✦—

Josey struggled to overcome her grogginess. She couldn't just sit there. She had to help, but she wasn't sure what she could do. The last thing she needed to do was get in the way. She watched Brad and Carry run toward Big Vern. In horror she watched Big Vern look up and then grab Rene tighter. He held the gun up to her head. "Don't come any closer. I will shoot her."

The two men backed off for the moment, not wanting to take any risks with Rene's life.

Brad's car, still running, was positioned next the driver's side of the van.

As Josey sat up she spotted Brad's backup gun stuck between the two front seats. Maria started to sit up, but Josey motioned for her to stay where she was. Josey reached over and grabbed the gun. Slowly and carefully, she opened the back door on the left side of the car. Shaking, she managed to slide like a snake quietly to the ground.

Josey was very nervous around guns. She'd had some bad experiences in the past with them. But her daughter's life was in jeopardy, and nothing would deter her from attempting to save Rene.

Slouched as low as possible, Josey moved around the car. A twig cracked under her foot. To Josey it sounded like a loud crackle. The sound seemed to permeate the dark, nighttime silence. She stopped and held her breath. Don't blow it now, Josey thought. She definitely didn't want to be the cause of any harm to Rene.

Big Vern appeared to have heard nothing.

Josey crouched as still as a statue for a few seconds longer just to be sure. Finally she stood, still motionless, near the van. Without warning, she felt a tap on her shoulder and a hand moving around her face to cover her mouth. Frozen, she looked around and saw Natasha.

Natasha put her finger to her mouth, forming a silent "shhh," and motioned to Josey to stay put.

Josey complied.

Natasha took the gun from Josey's hand. As she took the gun, Josey noticed another pistol secured in the strange woman's waistband.

Vern was obviously focused on escaping. He was concentrating on his grip on Rene. Josey watched his eyes move resolutely from Brad to Cary.

—◆—

Natasha, with the stealth of a ninja, worked her way to the side of the van while considering her options. She made it to the door on the driver's side and crouched just below the window.

The evening was warm, and Big Vern had left the window open while he was watching the house. The van was built in such a way that there was no passenger seat up front so the driver could get in and out on the passenger side.

—◆—

Brad and Cary, standing a safe distance from Vern, heard the twig crack and looked at each other.

"What?" Vern had observed their action, but fortunately, he must not have heard the noise himself. "Don't try anything," he said, tightening his grip on Rene. Rene's eyes bulged.

The two men caught a glimpse of Natasha as she sneaked silently around the vehicle and stayed still while Big Vern, holding the frightened Rene close to him, dragged her toward the van. Brad and Cary held their distance.

—✦—

Vern pulled Rene backwards and dragged her up the step into the van, her legs scraping the rough edges of the opening. In the absence of a front passenger seat, he forced Rene to the floor and climbed over her into the driver's seat.

The key was in the ignition. With the gun in one hand pointed at Rene, he made an awkward attempt to start the van with his other hand. The engine roared to life.

Without warning, as Vern fumbled with the gearshift, he felt a cold, hard cylinder press into the back of his head. "Let her go or I blow your stupid head off!" Natasha's thick accent accentuated her demand. Rene looked up at Natasha.

"She is my friend." Natasha cocked the gun, finger on the trigger. "Drop gun now!" she said, her voice sharp and convincing.

Big Vern dropped the gun.

Before Vern could react further, Brad flew into the van, pushed Rene into the backseat, and, without hesitation, punched Big Vern in the face. The sound of cartilage shattering echoed inside the vehicle as Vern's nose was smashed to the side of his face.

Ignoring the blood dripping over his mouth and chin, Vern managed to push his way out of the van. But he was surprised as Cary assaulted him, charging into him with the full force of his body.

—◆—

Vern, stunned only for a second, pushed Cary aside and kicked him hard in the stomach. Cary slumped over from the intense pain, but he got his bearings back quickly and rose up for another strike. He quickly realized that there was no gentle in this hulking giant.

Brad grabbed Big Vern's gun from the floor of the van and jumped to the ground to stand behind him. He slammed the gun into Vern's head. The blow jolted the big man off balance, and he fell hard onto the ground.

Wasting no time, Brad and Cary both jumped onto Vern and held him down.

—◆—

During the scuffle, Josey and Natasha rushed around to the other side of the van to Rene.

Fighting fatigue and fear, Josey gained a renewed surge of adrenaline, but she was trembling so hard that Natasha had to untie Rene's hands.

While Cary did his best to hold Vern down and pull his hands behind his back, Natasha threw Brad the rope she'd just removed from Rene. He quickly tied it around Vern's hands.

"This guy is huge! Hope this will hold him," cried Cary.

"Good work, Natasha—you too, Josey," Brad called to her. "Can you find something else we can use to tie his feet?"

"Rene, call the police while I get something," Josey said. Rene seemed to take a few seconds to gather herself, but she was soon running toward the house.

"Wait, Rene. Come back. Don't call the police," Brad said. "I'll give you a number to call."

Cary reached into his pocket, pulled out his tiny cell phone, and tossed it to Rene. "Here, use this," he said.

"5-5-5-4-3-5-5." Brad tossed out the numbers slowly so Rene could punch them into the phone. "His name is Mark," Brad said. "Tell him to come in the special van. And tell him to bring Jim and Pam."

Rene dialed the numbers, and a man answered the phone. She told him what Brad had said. He didn't ask why, only asked where. She gave him the address.

"Tell him to bring some medical supplies," Brad yelled.

"I heard him," Mark said. "We're on our way."

Josey limped into the house and found some packing tape, the kind that had reinforcing fiberglass filaments running through it. She ran back out, legs shaking, and gave it to Brad so he could secure his prisoner.

"This should hold him for a while," Cary said.

"Who is this guy?" Brad asked as he looked over at Josey. He had almost forgotten about Josey's injuries. She was a mess!

"His name is Big Vern. I heard them use that name at the clinic," Josey said. "He's the one who drugged me at the airport. There is so much to tell you. What a nightmare."

"Let's clean up this mess first. Then we'll talk." Brad eyes showed compassion as he noticed Josey unconsciously fingering her neck as if she was searching for her necklace.

Chapter 28

A large mobile unit, resembling a medium-size RV, pulled up in front of Josey's house in less than twenty minutes. Two burley men and one husky woman got out and ran over to the yard where Brad had Vern subdued.

"Guys, meet Mark, Jim, and Pam," Brad shouted, relieved to see his friends.

The two men immediately took charge of Vern. They needed the help of Brad and Cary to drag the massive man over to the van and pull him inside. They dropped a groggy Vern into a seat near the back of the van and immediately began to interrogate him.

—◆—

Pam, who looked to be in her early thirties, was a physician's assistant. Carrying a medical bag, she hurried into the house to attend to Josey and Rene. "You look like you've been hit by a car," Pam said as she scanned Josey's torso. Josey's knee needed stitches. Pam administered a local anesthetic to ease the pain and then did the stitching with the skill of an artist.

"Oh my God, here we go again." Josey was getting used to seeing part of her body being sewn up, but she still experienced small bursts of white flashes as she watched the needle going in and out of her damaged flesh.

Rene had incurred no further injuries, but Vern's roughness had exacerbated the old ones. He had severely wrenched her shoulder as he was forcing her into the van, and now the pain was almost unbearable. Pam helped Rene put her arm back in the sling and gave her a pill to help ease the pain.

—◆—

Brad left the van and went into the house. He had to move quickly before Vern's boss realized that his hit man had been brought down.

"Josey, I know you're tired and a little fuzzy, but did you get a chance to see anything at the clinic?"

"I think I witnessed more than I bargained for. I saw the people from San Salvador sedated in a large dorm in the clinic. I saw three dead people in a freezer in the lab." Josey told them what she'd seen and heard. "I almost

ended up on one of those slabs! I couldn't ..."
Josey stopped mid-sentence. "Oh, my God!"

"What?"

"Maria! The car ... quick ... the poor girl is still
in the car!" Josey jumped up, endangering the
new stitches.

Brad pushed her back. "Stay here, Josey." He
headed back to his car.

The motor was still running. He jumped into
the front seat and killed the motor, and then
he turned to see Maria huddled in a little ball
in the corner of the backseat, her face filled
with fear and anxiety.

"Maria, it's okay. Come with me." Brad got
out of the car and opened the rear door. He
held out his hand for her to join him. As they
walked, he touched her elbow with a gentle
nudge and directed her back into Josey's
house.

Everyone looked up and stared at a timid
Maria as she entered the room. Streaks of
dried tears marred her pretty face.

"Pam, please take a look at her. She has some
abrasions." Josey walked up to them and took
Maria from Brad's grip. "Don't worry, Maria,"
she said. "You're okay here. You're safe."

Maria nodded and sat down so that Pam could tend to her wounds—just some minor cuts and bruises.

"I'll make some tea," Cary said as he moved to the kitchen.

"Forget the tea," said Josey. "There's some brandy in the cabinet—pour us all a glass."

Brad gestured a "not me" with a wave of his hand. "We need to get to the bottom of this. Maybe Maria can shed some light for us."

Maria looked up when she heard her name. "Are you going to send me back?"

"No, Maria. We want to help, but we need to know what you were doing at the clinic." Brad tried not to intimidate her.

"I come to United States to work. To get money for my family in San Salvador. I just arrive—on the same bus as Miss Josey. I sit next to her, and she was asleep. Something wasn't right—I could feel it." She looked at Josey. "Then they put us in a clinic with doctors and nurses. They gave us pills and put us in the big room for sleep. I was scared."

Cary walked back into the room and handed each of the women a glass of brandy and lifted his own to his lips.

Natasha followed with a tray full of light snacks. "You must have some food. Eat now." They looked at Natasha.

—◆—

How does she do that? Josey thought, starting to really enjoy having Natasha and her gourmet skills around. She also felt safer having seen Natasha in action.

Maria accepted the glass, grabbed a small finger sandwich, and continued. "I see Miss Josey peek in my room tonight so I follow her."

"I don't think she knows anything, Brad. She got there the same time I did," Josey said.

"Just wait, Josey. She might shed a little light on this." He turned to Maria. "Weren't you a little suspicious when they put you in that dorm with the others?" Brad asked.

"It was night. They said for us to get our rest and we would move on in the morning. The others were already asleep. But it was strange that nobody wake up when we arrive."

Brad agreed with Josey. "We'll try to find out what we can from the big guy, but I don't think he'll say much. We need to find out who the American connection is. It has to be someone at Viscount."

"I've been thinking about that, and I have an idea," Josey interrupted. "I think you're right, there has to be a tie to someone at Viscount. The clues seem to be lining up—the cigarettes, the logbook notations, flights from El Salvador, and what I saw at the clinic. Why don't I try to set up a meeting with Tony McIntyre tomorrow and see what I can dig up? He's probably wondering why I haven't gotten back to him anyway."

Josey was exhausted, but she was able to muster up enough energy for one more task that night—or that morning; it was almost five o'clock. The sun would soon be rising.

Josey knew it was too early to reach Tony at his office, but she was glad because she really didn't want to speak to him yet in person anyway. So she called his number and left an urgent message on his voicemail telling him she wanted to see him at four thirty that afternoon to discuss some new and important developments in the Cisco case. Unless she heard otherwise, she'd be at his office.

Josey hung up the phone and turned to Maria. "Come with me." She led her to the guest room. "You can stay in here." She showed Maria the bathroom and pulled a nightshirt out of the closet and handed it to her. Maria accepted it graciously and stood by the bed as Josey said goodnight and shut the door behind her.

Josey looked at Brad, "Maybe she'll remember something after she calms down some and has a good night's sleep," she said.

Brad sent Cary and Rene home and escorted Josey into her bedroom. He sat her down on the bed and gave her a tender kiss on the lips, his hands softly touching her cheeks. Josey felt an old familiar stir within her, one she often tried to push back to the recesses of her mind and body. She knew he was feeling it too. She touched her wedding ring and wondered if maybe it was finally time to put it away. But they both held back, as usual. This time they were both too tired to discuss it.

"Josey, get some rest. This is going to be another tough day, and you'll need all the strength you can muster."

"Okay. Will you stay?"

"Sure. Your faithful protector is at your service."

Josey smiled at him, a thankful smile.

Brad smiled back with a look that implied, "Don't worry. I'll always be there for you." Then, in his own enigmatic way, he gazed at her and said, "You stink!"

"What! How rude!" Josey looked into the mirror and caught a glimpse of her reflection. She looked ghastly. Then she laughed. "I get your drift. Thanks for being so delicate about it." She got up and went into the bathroom to take a long, hot shower. Her body would never be the same after all she'd been through that night—especially being stuck in that appalling men's restroom. She could still sense the feeling of that vile bug crawling up her leg. She stood under the shower for a long time, scrubbing and scrubbing her body until it was almost raw, while still trying to be gentle around the stitches, multiple bruises, and scratches.

Josey dried her hair, put on the softest nightgown she could find, set her alarm for three o'clock in the afternoon, and dropped into the bed. She was out like a light.

—◆—

After seeing that Josey was safely settled, Brad went back to the van. "Well, what do we have so far?" he enquired as he glared down at Vern, who was slumped over, wedged into a small seat in the back of the van. Vern stared ahead; blue veins bulged in his thick neck.

"So far the big guy's got lockjaw," Jim replied.

"Yeah, but he'll come around—we'll see to that," said Mark

Brad knew that they would eventually get him to talk. He was certain they would find that Big Vern's fingerprints matched those on Josey's car and the cigarette butt she'd found in her yard.

"Where's his stuff?" Brad asked.

"This is everything." Jim pointed to a small stack of items sitting on a console near the front of the van.

Brad eyed the items. "No license. No ID. This is it?" Not much—a few bucks and a packet of the infamous, smelly cigarettes with a matchbook stuck in the cellophane lining. Brad pulled the matchbook out. The logo was printed in Spanish. On the flap was a picture of a restaurant in El Salvador—La Taverna del Sol. He remembered seeing that name in the Cisco logbooks when he was trying to help Josey uncover clues. He looked at the matchbook carefully. There it was, clear as day: Proprietario—Alberto Murillo. "AM."

"Hmmm, Alberto Murillo," Brad said casually, all the while viewing Vern carefully out of the corner of his eye. He saw a slight twitch in Vern's face. He was right—Murillo was involved. "So, big guy, you know the man— this fellow Murillo?" Brad said.

Vern just glared at him.

"Just what I thought." Brad gave Vern a sly look and turned to Mark and Jim. "He knows him all right."

"Mark," Brad handed him the matchbook. "Check this out. I think we might have found an accomplice."

"Sure, I'll get right on it. Should have something for you in a couple of hours."

"Go ahead. Take him away." Brad waved a sign of dismissal. "Get some rest and call me later in the morning," he continued.

Mark and the other two agents got back into the van and left.

While Brad was watching them drive away, he noticed that his car was still partially blocking the street.

"Geez—I don't believe it. What a night!" He got in and moved the car into Josey's driveway.

Brad walked back into Josey's house and decided to check on her one last time. He stood in her bedroom doorway casting a reflective eye on her sleeping figure. He couldn't imagine what life would be like without Josey.

Brad left the door cracked open slightly and went into the living room. A wave of exhaustion overcame him as he lowered himself onto the sofa. He wasn't about to leave her alone until he knew she'd be safe. He was asleep within seconds.

Chapter 29

Tony McIntyre checked his messages first thing when he arrived at his office. He was baffled by Josey's phone message. He sensed the urgency in her voice and was curious to see what she had to say—so much so that he cancelled a meeting to free up the time for her.

—◆—

The Viscount corporate offices were located on one of the perimeter roads that bordered the DFW airport, which meant they were close to Josey's house. She was glad the office was nearby since she had slept until the last minute and had had just enough time to make herself presentable for the meeting.

Brad had still been there when she got up, and Maria was now sitting quietly at the kitchen table sipping a soft drink.

Josey looked over at her. "Maria, you can stay here until we figure out what is going on. You'll be safe."

"My friends. I think they are not safe," Maria said, unable again to hold back the tears.

"While I'm gone, try to remember anything you saw or heard, and when I return, we'll do whatever we can to help your friends," Josey said.

The three of them watched while Natasha threw together another gourmet grilled cheese sandwich—creamy cheeses nobody could name melted between two thick slices of brioche.

—◆—

While Josey ate, Brad briefed her for her meeting with Tony. He was concerned about sending her out there alone, but he knew that it was the only way to get inside.

"I heard from Mark this morning," Brad said.

"What did he say? Any leads?"

"Not yet, but he's still working on it. If anyone can pull up dirt, it's Mark." He looked at Josey. "Josey, I'm not letting you go alone. I'll follow you over to the Viscount offices and wait for you at the Café Auberge, that new little restaurant on Route 183, just west as you leave the airport. It's a nice quiet place." He gave her arm a gentle squeeze. "Call me as soon as you're finished with McIntyre and then come on over to the restaurant. We can discuss your meeting and decide what to do next." He retrieved a small shopping bag from the counter and handed it to her. "Here, I ran to the store and picked up a new earpiece for your cell phone you while you were asleep." He knew she would be lost without that bit of technology. "And I've charged your phone. Remember, all you have to do is punch one for me."

Josey smiled. "You think of everything. Thanks."

"If you sense the slightest danger, call me right away."

Maria watched as Josey left the house with Brad following.

They found the Viscount building with no trouble. Brad watched Josey go into the building before he continued on to the restaurant to wait for her.

—◆—

Josey had arrived right on time. She checked in at the visitor's desk. While waiting for her visitor's badge, she was too nervous at first to see the figure of a man moving through the rear of the lobby.

— ✦ —

But Royce Allemand noticed her. As he glanced around the lobby, he spotted a vaguely familiar-looking woman across the room. After a second careful look, he knew it was Josey. Although Allemand knew she wouldn't recognize him, he hurried through the lobby and down the hall.

— ✦ —

That sound! Josey heard it again—step, thud, step, thud. She stood stiff for a second then looked around the lobby. The man with the limp was gone. She was sure it was the same one. Did he see me? she thought. Should I ask the receptionist about him? Am I safe here? She felt a knot growing in her stomach.

— ✦ —

Allemand was stunned. How could she possibly be here? How did she get away? Why didn't someone contact me? What is she doing here?

Trying to avoid attention, he walked as quickly as possible to his office, shut his door, and grabbed the phone. This time he didn't take precautions. He didn't care that he was at work. There was no time to go out and find another phone booth.

"Murillo, did you know she escaped?" Allemand was hissing hysterically. "How did you let that happen? Where's Big Vern?" he shouted. "She never saw me and can't recognize me now, but what if she can put this together. What should I do?"

"Stop it! Let me talk," Murillo demanded. "It happened late last night. She got away. I'm working on it. That's all. We can't find a trace of Big Vern. He never came back, but don't worry about him. He can take care of himself. Just stay calm. She doesn't know anything about you. You would know by now if anyone was on to you. Besides, this is good news—at least now we know where she is. Next time she won't be so lucky!"

—✦—

Tony McIntyre walked into the lobby and greeted Josey. His stare was obvious. "Good grief—look at you. You look ... oh, I'm sorry. That was rude. What happened to you? Were you in an accident or something?" Tony's concern seemed genuine.

"It looks worse than it is. Just a little spill, that's all," Josey said, trying to play down the injuries.

"Josey, your message sounded so urgent. Is everything okay? Please, let's go into my office. You want something to drink?"

"No thanks," Josey said as she once more looked around intently while they walked. She was half hoping she'd spot the man with the limp—and half hoping that she wouldn't.

He took her into a bright, spacious corner office with a small conference table at one end that had room for about six people. There were windows on two sides of the office. The largest windows overlooked the DFW airport where one could see the constant flow of airplanes taking off and landing.

Tony was a tidy man—for a lawyer. His casework was neatly stacked in straight rows. Josey knew only one other person who was that organized—one of her best friends, whom she often called for assistance when working on various cases.

Tony motioned for her to sit down at the conference table. Josey pulled out her notepad and some copies of a draft report she'd prepared. "Thanks for dropping everything to see me, Tony," she began. "I don't want you to think I'm overreacting, but this case has taken a turn, and there are some things that you need to know about. What I'm about to tell you is bizarre." Tony was nothing but attentive, so she continued, "When I was reviewing Bobby's logbooks, I noticed he was logging his flight engineer time as copilot time. He also made some weird notes in the margins while he was on his trips to San Salvador. The worst part," she added, "was that my house was broken into. Nothing was taken, and I could only assume the break-in had to with those logbooks.

Before she could go on, a man she hadn't seen before suddenly opened the door to the office. "Oh, excuse me," said the man as he briskly took several steps into the room—step, thud. "I didn't know you were in a meeting. I'm sorry." Without waiting for an invitation, Allemand advanced farther into the room.

A chill ran up Josey's neck. She recognized the voice—and the limp. He was one of the men from the clinic—the ones who wanted her dead. She tried to keep calm and appear nonchalant, but it wasn't easy trying not to show any indication that she recognized him.

"Oh, Josey, this is Royce Allemand, our vice president of operations. Royce, Josey is the expert I was telling you about. She's working on the Cisco case. We're going over some of the discrepancies she found. Seems like Bobby wasn't totally honest about his flying experience, and he often took risks when he was flying."

—◆—

"Really?" Royce said with indifference. "Anything you can do to save the company money." Obviously, she wasn't telling it all, he was thinking. There had to be something in those documents that had led her to discovering the clinic. He had to find out. In the meantime, he had to deal with Josey again.

— ✦ —

It's him—RA! Josey thought, terrified at being in the same room with a potential killer. She needed to get out of there as soon as possible.

Josey's cell phone vibrated against her side. She jumped. It scared her half to death.

"What is it?" Tony asked. He'd obviously observed Josey's startled expression.

Josey pulled her cell phone out of her jacket pocket. "Nothing—just my cell phone. I have it on vibrate and forgot that it was in my coat pocket. It just startled me."

She looked at the caller ID. It was from Rene. She'd call her back after the meeting. She dropped the phone back into her pocket.

Josey wasn't sure just how much she wanted to tell Tony at this point and was glad that she hadn't gone over more details with him.

Her primary goal now was to get out of the Viscount offices quickly so she could get the information back to Brad as soon as possible.

"Look here," Josey said as she handed Allemand a sheet of paper that contained a few notes on the flight discrepancies. She tried not to let her hands shake as he took the papers and glanced nonchalantly at the remarks.

—◆—

"Good work," Royce said. "Well, look at the time. It was a pleasure meeting you, Josey." He handed the piece of paper back and excused himself. He hadn't noticed anything of significance on the papers. Maybe she really didn't know anything.

—◆—

Josey went over a few more notes with Tony and tried to wrap things up quickly. "I guess that about covers it for now," she told him. "I really thought you needed to know about this. I'm a little nervous about the break-in. If you can think of anything that might shed light on discovering who it was, I'd really appreciate your help. The police haven't been able to come up with anything."

"I'll do everything I can to help," Tony said.

"By the way, Josey, we neglected to get a copy of the logbooks. Do you think you can make us a copy and get it to us? Or just give them to us and we'll make the copy and return yours to you."

"Sure, I'll take care of it, Tony."

Chapter 30

As Josey was leaving Tony's office, she pulled her cell phone from her pocket, changed the setting from vibrate to ring, stuck the tiny wireless earpiece into her left ear, and checked for messages. She had one message from Rene, who wanted to let her know that Annie Cisco had called. Annie seemed anxious to talk to her about some information she had about Bobby.

Josey would call Annie back, but first she had to speak to Brad.

She punched one—Brad's speed dial number—and dropped the phone back into her left jacket pocket to free up her hands. She headed for her car. It was after five, and the lot was almost empty.

—◆—

"Josey?" Brad answered on the first ring after seeing her name show up on the screen. Several patrons in the restaurant turned and glared at him. He understood. It bugged him too when he heard the continuous beeping of cell

257

phones—and the following conversations—as he was trying to enjoy a leisurely meal.

"Josey, you done with the meeting so soon?" he said softly. He didn't need to whisper. Other people in the restaurant spoke normally—what difference did it make that he was talking to air?

"Brad, you won't believe this. It was all I could do to keep from passing out on the spot. It was him—the guy who was at the clinic. I recognized his voice and his limp—RA. It's Royce Allemand, a vice president at Viscount. Can you believe it?" She struggled to keep her voice from shaking. "Just as I realized who it was, my cell phone started to vibrate and scared the wits out of me."

"Calm down and tell me," Brad said.

—◆—

"Okay, I need to get out of here fast. I'm on my way over to the restaurant." She rushed to her car as she continued to talk to Brad.

"Brad, I don't want to seem paranoid, but I'm really worried now. I don't think Allemand knows that I suspect him of being involved in anything, but he obviously thinks I know something." She reached her car. "Hold on, Brad. I'm at my car. I need to find my keys.

Don't hang up."

—✦—

"I'm not going anywhere." Brad could sense the anxiety in her voice. He stayed on the line.

"Darn, I can't believe it. I left it unlocked!" Josey said. "I have got to get a hold of myself. I'm getting careless."

Brad, still on the line, straightened up. "Wait, Josey!" he jumped up from his seat and yelled. "No! Don't open the door!" The people in the restaurant all turned to look at him.

—✦—

But Brad's warning came too late. Josey was already sitting in the front seat. She was about to shut the door when she felt something sharp stick into her right side.

She looked down and saw the polished glint of a steel blade. She froze.

A small man started speaking with a Spanish accent. "Just be quiet and start the car. I'll tell you where to go." He was just behind her to the right, crouching low in the backseat.

Josey hesitated.

"Do it!" he demanded.

Visibly shaken, Josey fumbled around with the keys.

"Look, lady. Stop wasting time. Get this car going, now!"

— ✦ —

Brad listened to the drama as it was unfolding. He threw some money on the table without even looking to see how much and ran from the restaurant, apologizing to customers as he pushed them aside to hasten his departure. He jumped in his car and started the motor preparing to drive toward the Viscount offices.

"Stay calm, Josey," Brad said as coolly as possible. "Try not to let him know you're on the phone. I'm heading that way now. Don't get brave on me, girl. Just do as he says," Brad cautioned.

— ✦ —

Josey fumbled some more, trying to delay the departure as much as possible, hoping Brad could catch up with them.

"Come on, lady." The little man pressed the knife more harshly at her side. It felt as if it had cut through her clothes, but hadn't broken the skin.

She finally got the keys in the ignition and started the car. "I'm sorry—what do you expect? You have a knife stuck in my side. I'm trying! I'm trying!" She took a deep breath. "Where are we going?"

"Go south to the airport exit and get on one eighty-three west," he said. "Don't try nothing," he demanded.

"One eighty-three west?" she repeated.

Josey looked up into her rear view mirror and noticed that an unfamiliar car had pulled out behind her as she had turned out of the parking lot. The car stayed close behind.

"There's someone following us—an old black Mustang. Is he with you?" she said.

"Shut up and drive." She could see him glance quickly behind them. "Speed up!"

"It's rush hour—what do you expect me to do? What are you going to do with me? Why are you doing this?" Josey's hands were shaking on the steering wheel.

"Another word, and I'll use this knife to cut out your tongue!" He waved the knife up at her face and quickly moved it back to her side.

Josey got the message.

They drove for about ten miles before he spoke again. "Now turn on eight twenty."

"Eight twenty north or south?" she asked.

"Go right."

"Right, okay."

—◆—

"Thank God I was close," Brad said out loud. He caught up with her SUV, which was moving at a moderate speed several cars in front of him. He spotted the Mustang that was following Josey and her abductor.

"Okay, Josey," Brad said quietly. "I'm behind you. Don't panic."

—◆—

The knowledge of Brad's close presence gave her a sense of relief. Suddenly, she started hearing small beeps in her ear. Oh no, not now! she thought. The phone was dying—her battery was going dead, and she couldn't do anything. She prayed that Brad wouldn't lose them.

She hoped that Brad had heard the beeps too. "Josey, cough if you can hear me." Brad said.

She coughed and thought, I should have a few more minutes left. She looked behind and saw the old Mercedes a few cars back.

"Okay, lady, turn off here."

They got off the freeway and turned left under a bridge going west on to a two-lane road that led into an undeveloped area northwest of Fort Worth. The city was behind, and the area was rustic and barren, reminding her of a scene in an old western movie.

— ◆ —

Brad had to be careful now. He watched closely to see if the men were onto him. Brad was trained in these tactics and used his experience to his advantage, staying a safe distance away.

There weren't many cars on the road, and the likelihood of being spotted increased, but the abductors obviously weren't pros at being elusive, and Brad was betting that the two men were totally unaware that help for their captive was close by.

"Turn there," Josey's abductor ordered. "Stop—over there—go slow. Stop now."

Josey pulled into an empty dirt lot next to an abandoned grain processing plant. An old, empty grain elevator—obviously inoperative for years—stood off to the side.

The Mustang that had been following along behind them pulled up. Another small Hispanic man got out and rushed over to Josey's car. He was carrying a black metal device the size of a small alarm clock.

— ✦ —

The sun had found its way below the horizon in the west. The lights of the city were dim, and the dark countryside looked ominous. Still sitting in the car, Josey felt cold sweat dripping from her neck moistening the tips of her hair. She could hear her heart pumping in her ears.

"Manuel, I have it here," said the man from the Mustang. Let me know when you're ready."

"Just a minute, Fernando," said the man in Josey's car. "I need to take care of her first."

"What is he holding? What are you going to do with me?" demanded Josey. Neither of them answered. "What do you want—my money? Take it!" She knew they didn't want her money. It was clear they were being paid to get rid of her. "How much are they paying you? I can give you more. That is a bomb. I know it." She pointed to the device. "You don't have to do this. Let me go, and I promise not to say anything."

Josey had caught their names, but what was the difference? There were thousands of men called Fernando and Manuel in Texas.

"Shut up!" Manuel wasn't going to tell her anything. With his right hand still holding the knife to her side, he reached into his pocket with his left hand and pulled out a hypodermic needle. He yelled at Fernando, "Get over here!"

—◆—

While Brad was following the two cars, he'd called Mark—he knew he would need backup. Mark and his team were on the way. He thought about all the favors he had asked of Mark. He would be paying that team back for a long time.

Brad had held back as he watched the two cars pull into the parking lot of the deserted plant. He continued to drive a few hundred yards, and then he pulled off the road behind an old deserted trailer—probably the plant office. It was obvious that the place hadn't been in operation for many years.

Brad got out of the car and hurried back toward the grain elevator, staying out of sight.

—✦—

Josey turned to look at her assailant. Just as she opened her mouth to speak, Manuel dropped the knife, grabbed her head, and started to thrust the needle in the side of her neck.

"Oh, no—not again!" Josey jolted sideways knocking the needle from his hand.

"You bitch!" Manuel leaned over to pick it up.

Josey grabbed her purse by the strap and swung it as hard as she could it at his head. After struggling with the handle, she managed to get the car door open. She jumped out of the car and started to run, but Fernando grabbed her and pulled her back to the car. He put the little black device on the ground gently so he could hold Josey with two hands while Manuel finally managed to get the needle firmly into her neck.

In seconds, Josey was unconscious.

—✦—

Manuel pulled the needle away and pushed her back into the car—the backseat this time. As Josey fell over, Manuel spotted the earpiece. He yanked it out and realized what it was. "What the ...!" he yelled. He looked around for the phone and saw the bulge in

Josey's pocket. He ripped the pocket as he pulled the phone out and noticed it was still turned on. He hit disconnect. "Hurry up, Fernando. Someone was listening to us," said Manuel. "Whoever it is can't know who we are, but he might know where we are. The lady was repeating my directions while we were driving. Get the bomb in place and let's get out of here!" he screamed to Fernando.

Fernando placed the device under the SUV. The two men jumped into the Mustang and took off.

"Wait until we get down the road a ways and then hit the detonator," ordered Manuel, panic in his voice.

—◆—

Brad was almost to her car, but he was still hidden in the shadow of the building when he saw the two men jump into the idling Mustang. Their wheels sprayed up a cloud of dust as they took off.

Brad ran as fast as he could to the passenger side of the SUV, which was facing away from the road. He pulled Josey's limp body out of the car and carried her toward the building.

Just seconds later, when they were only several yards from the car, the impact from the explosion knocked him off his feet and sent Josey flying from his arms to the ground.

—◆—

Manuel and Fernando smiled as they looked back and saw a giant flash as the car exploded sending smoke and flames into the sky.

—◆—

Brad brushed the dust off his face and got his bearings. Still a little shaky, his ears ringing, he ran over to Josey, who was lying unconscious against the building. He checked her over to see if she'd incurred any serious injuries from the explosion or the fall, and couldn't see anything. Then he lifted her with both arms and carried her to his car, careful not to aggravate her wounds as he lay her on the backseat. "Déjà vu," he whispered to himself.

Brad's friend Mark arrived shortly after the blast. Before any emergency vehicles were on the scene, Brad made sure that the agency would take care of the cleanup and guide the news coverage. It was critical to the case that Allemand and his group believed that Josey had died in that blast.

Josey was still out cold, and Brad needed to attend to her immediately. He didn't know what they'd used to drug her, but he figured it couldn't be fatal since it appeared they wanted people to think she'd died in the blast.

He drove her to a special clinic near his home where the doctors could be trusted to maintain silence. The doctor checked her carefully. "She's a lucky lady," he said. "No broken bones or serious lacerations. I can't tell about concussion, since she's still out from the drug—which by the way was just a strong sedative. She'll be okay from that." He continued, "I don't see any nasty bumps on her head, so I don't think you have to worry, but keep a close eye on her anyway." The doctor looked at Josey and back at Brad, "Is this woman accident prone? I see indications of other injuries, lacerations, stitches, and bruises. They seem to be fresh but not from this accident."

Brad responded by shaking his head with resignation and saying, "I'm starting to believe she is."

Brad took Josey to his house where he knew she'd be safe.

Chapter 31

The next morning when Josey woke up, she was startled to find herself in Brad's bedroom wearing one of his large T-shirts.

She was relieved to see Brad walk into the bedroom. He sat down on the edge of the bed. She sat upright as he pulled her close, put his arms around her, and gave her a light kiss on the mouth before he backed off. The warmth of his affection soothed her aching body, and she was again aware of feelings she had been repressing for a long time. "What happened? The last thing I remember was someone sticking me with a needle. What is it with these people and their drugs? Can't they be more creative?" He just hugged her again.

"Brad." She thought about the kiss and her face felt flushed. "You're always there for me. I sure make your life challenging, don't I?"

"That is the year's biggest understatement." It wasn't really a question. This was becoming routine for Brad.

"My kids—do they know I'm okay? They'll freak."

"Yeah, I called them on the way home. They're okay."

"What about Maria?" she asked.

"Pam went back to your house. She's questioning her now. We're trying to find out more about the situation at the clinic. She doesn't know what happened to you yet. We'll keep her sequestered until we decide what to do."

A familiar voice came from the doorway. "Here, you eat now." Josey looked over at the door to Brad's bedroom to see Natasha entering with a tray full of breakfast foods.

"Natasha?" She looked at Brad.

"Yeah, I called her. She was concerned about you. I knew some of her famous beignets and French chicory coffee would perk you up." He grinned from ear to ear.

"Natasha, you and your cooking are really starting to grow on me. You might have to stay on permanently."

Brad turned the TV on and switched to the local news station. As he clicked through the channels, they noticed that every one of them was broadcasting the incident. The news anchors reported that the police had found one body in the rubble and were in the process of determining the identity. Pictures of the decimated vehicle filled the screen.

"I'm lucky to be alive." Josey winced as she viewed the scene.

"You can say that again. You can thank your kids for making you wear that little earpiece."

"You can say that again."

"Are you feeling up to discussing the case now?" Brad asked.

"I'm a little foggy, but this coffee should cure that," she said.

"Good. Get dressed and come into the kitchen. Here, you can wear my robe." He pointed to where he had put it at the end of the bed. "Mark and Jim are here. We can probably use Natasha too. First, we need to find out why those documents you have are so important and just what is going on in that clinic."

"Speaking of Natasha, you keep putting me off when I ask about her. I'm sure there is more to her than her amazing skills as a chef."

"Later," he said as he walked out, closing the door behind him.

Josey was stiff as she got out of the bed. She slipped into Brad's robe and made her way into the kitchen.

Brad, Mark, and Jim were sitting at the table drinking coffee and trying to determine their next course of action. Natasha was passing out more beignets along with giant blueberry muffins.

Mark started as Josey slipped gingerly into a kitchen chair. "You were right about Murillo. He has been under surveillance in Central America for about a year," he said. "US immigration agents believe he's involved in some shady dealings transporting Salvadorians into the US illegally, but they haven't been able to pin him with anything yet."

"Did you learn anything from Big Vern?" Josey asked.

"Nothing yet," Brad said. "But we need to focus on the clinic now." He went back to the subject of Murillo. "Murillo must have some involvement with the clinic. They could be using it as a processing point."

"What about the bodies?" Josey asked.

"I don't know. That's what we need to find out," Brad replied.

"When I was at the clinic, I saw video cameras all over the place," Josey said. "They must have me on videotape because I heard them mention something about seeing my picture. If you could get hold of the tapes, they might have pictures of Allemand going there and who knows what else? They must keep the footage for a while. I sort of know the layout of the building. Maybe I can help." She already knew what Brad's comeback would be.

"You're nuts, girl. I'm not letting you go back over there!"

"With Big Vern gone, their security might not be as tight," she said. "They didn't catch me right away when I left with Maria that night. I think the security room was the one next to the first room they put me in. I'm sure I heard some muffled voices in that room and in the hall as they exited."

"You just try to draw me a diagram of the place," said Brad. "Let us handle it from here."

Josey made some sketches. Her drawing skills were horrible, but she was sure they would help the others get a feel for how the rooms and halls were laid out.

"We have someone watching the clinic now," Jim said. "We found out that Murillo is in town. He flew in on a private jet into Addison Airport. The plane is still there. But he hasn't shown up at the clinic yet."

Brad's cell phone rang, and he jumped up to answer it. Everyone stopped and watched.

"Yeah." Brad nodded. He just listened for a while and finally said, "Okay, you stay there and let me know if you come up with anything else." He disconnected the call. "That was Pam. Maria doesn't know much. She had just got to the clinic herself, but she said that everyone who was brought in with her was being held in the same room, and there were four others already in the room when they got there. She said they were told they'd been brought there to work, but she thought something wasn't right because, as soon as they arrived, the doctors and nurses came in and started drawing their blood and conducting all kinds of medical tests on them." After a pause he said, "Her brother was part of the group. She's afraid for his safety."

"We have to get those people out of there, Brad," Josey said.

"I know. Let's get back to the plan."

"If we can get hold of tapes with Murillo and Allemand together, and get pictures of the inside of the clinic," said Mark, "we may have all we need to implicate them. We need to get hold of the records at the clinic before they're all destroyed."

"We'll go back this evening," Brad said. Mark and Jim left to make preparations.

Chapter 32

"Come on," said Josey. "You have to let me go with you. With the four of us, we can get in and out quicker. I can do it!" Josey had been pleading with Brad, Mark, and Jim to let her join the search party when they returned to the clinic. Brad had been obstinately objecting, but Josey finally convinced him that having her there would enable them to move more quickly through the building.

— ✦ —

Mark and Jim drove the agency van to Brad's house where they picked up Brad and Josey and headed east. The van was equipped with sophisticated surveillance equipment and other technology. They were prepared for just about any situation. All four were dressed in black and looked like burglars about to rob a bank. Fortunately, Brad had been able to outfit Josey from his closet.

They arrived at the clinic at quarter to four in the morning. The sky was still dark; a thick cloud cover blocked out the almost-full moon.

Brad, Josey, and Mark were wearing the latest wireless communication equipment. Jim would monitor them from the van and relay any important information as necessary. His position also served as a precaution; he could organize help quickly in case one of them got into trouble.

There were only a couple of cars in the parking lot. Mark parked the van in an area that provided a limited view of the clinic. They sat still and observed the facility for about fifteen minutes. Everything seemed quiet enough.

Brad, Josey, and Mark silently slipped from the van and went around to the back of the building. They spotted the surveillance camera and watched it as it spanned the parking lot. One by one, they went over the fence, the two men assisting Josey. They kept a keen eye on the security camera, and when all was clear, they headed for the back door that Josey and Maria had used when they made their escape.

Mark did his magic with the keypad to disarm the alarm and opened the door in less than a minute. He checked the hallway. It was vacant. He took the lead with Josey close behind him to lead the way while Brad followed.

The hallway was eerily quiet. They all seemed to hold their breath as they moved in silence through the facility.

Josey pointed to the lab. Mark slipped into the room, his camera ready to photograph the bodies and any other evidence of foul play he could find.

— ✦ —

Josey found the security office. Brad turned the door handle, opened the door a crack, and peered in. A small, chubby black man was sitting in a chair with his back to the door and his feet propped up on the desk. A row of monitors was arranged on a long table in front of him.

The security guard didn't move. A closer look revealed that he was asleep, his face tilted forward, with his chin touching his chest. They could hear him snoring lightly.

Brad motioned for Josey to leave. She'd served her purpose and needed to get out of there as quickly as possible.

Josey stood in the doorway watching.

"Go!" he formed the word with his lips and waved her away again.

Josey complied.

—✦—

Before the guard had a chance to awaken, Brad quickly pulled a wide elastic band from his pack and secured it around the man's head, immobilizing his mouth. As the man began to stir, Brad retrieved a set of zip tie disposable handcuffs from his pocket and secured the guard's hands behind his back. Then he tied the man's feet with another zip tie and dragged him to corner of the room out of sight from anyone who might walk into the door. All of this took mere seconds.

Brad looked into the man's bulging eyes, put his fingers to his lips, and pointed to his gun to let the man know that any noise would be his last. The man tried to speak, so Brad pulled the elastic gag away from his mouth, urging him to be quiet. "Look, man," said the guard. "I'm just a temp employee. I don't know nothin' about anything here."

Brad thought, This security guard isn't one of Murillo's thugs. He's just an ordinary man who needs a night job. I don't think he's likely to jeopardize his life for this minimum-wage job. The way the guard's body was shaking uncontrollably confirmed his assumption. Brad imagined he must be praying for his life at the moment. He couldn't take any chances, though, and he put the gag back into the man's mouth. He turned away and began downloading security images onto flash drives.

—✦—

Meanwhile, Josey headed down the corridor to return the way she had come in. Without warning, she heard footsteps in the corridor down the hall and to the left. She froze for an instant and looked left and right for a place to hide. She knew she couldn't retrace her steps. She slipped around the corner. She had no choice but to enter the closest room. Luckily, the door wasn't locked.

Josey opened the door just enough to let herself in. She closed it behind her without making any noise. She turned around and pressed her back to the wall next to the door.

She looked into the room. A dim florescent light from under a shelf cast an eerie glow across stacks of containers that looked like overly-fancy picnic coolers, each with a silver label denoting the contents: heart, liver .... She was horrified, and her knees buckled. She reached out for something to support her. Finding nothing close, she simply lowered herself to the floor and sat with her knees pressed up against her chest. She could barely believe what she was seeing, but it all began to fit together. Pax 1 and Pax 2? They were bodies. She realized that Murillo and Allemand weren't just transporting undocumented citizens from San Salvador for cheap labor; they were killing them for their organs. She thought about poor little Maria. Bile rose in Josey's throat, and she had to take several deep breaths to keep from vomiting.

— ◆ —

In the middle of the night, Allemand had come back to the clinic. Fearful of being exposed, he had decided to get rid of any evidence that might link Murillo or him to the conspiracy. Carrying a large leather bag, he entered the executive office where he and Murillo had often discussed their transactions. First he opened the safe that contained stacks of one-hundred-dollar bills. He grabbed as much as his satchel could hold. Just as he was thrashing through files to find anything that could link the operation to himself or Viscount, he thought he heard some noises outside the office. Having found no records, he grabbed his bag and opened the door enough to see if anyone was in the hallway. The coast looked clear, so he took off down the hall toward the exit.

Chapter 33

Brad finished searching the security room and silently slipped out toward the exit. Near the exit he met Mark who, having followed Josey's directions, was trying to lead five frightened, but silent, prisoners quietly through the corridors. The other captives were not in any kind of shape to be moved quickly, as they were heavily sedated. The rescue team would have to call for help to retrieve them as soon as possible.

Jim met the group at the van and directed the young men and women to get in. He looked around and back at Mark and Brad.

"Where's Josey?" Mark asked.

"I thought she was still with you." Jim tapped his headset. "I haven't heard a peep from her for the last few minutes." He rushed back into the van to his monitoring equipment.

—✦—

Josey, still crouching against the wall, heard another sound. She looked up to see the doorknob turning slowly. She naturally assumed it was Brad coming to get her so they could leave.

—◆—

Just after Allemand had left his office, he heard another slight noise in the hall. He turned the corner just in time to see the door to the organ room shut. He reached into a side pocket of the leather bag and pulled out a small handgun.

—◆—

Josey turned as the door to the organ room opened. She looked up in disbelief at the face of Royce Allemand. He, in turn, stared at her in disbelief. "It's you! I—I thought you were dead!" he stammered. He lifted his gun and pointed it straight into Josey's face. Then he reached down and grabbed her arm, his fingers so tight they almost broke the skin. He yanked her up and dragged her out into the hall.

"There are agents everywhere," Josey said. "Please don't point that gun at me. You should give up. Maybe they can cut a deal with you." She attempted with all her might to maintain her composure. She knew she had to bide her time, and she hoped that Jim would hear her and send support.

"You're like a recurring nightmare," Allemand said. "This time, though, the dream is going to end—for good."

Josey stared at the two protruding purple veins pulsating on his forehead. He was a loose cannon; she needed to be careful.

"Get going." He shoved her hard along the hall. She thought they were headed toward an outside door. "We're getting out of here, and you're coming with me as insurance. Unbuckle your belt," he demanded as he pointed his gun at her waist.

"What?"

"Unbuckle it. Do it!" He poked her this time.

Josey did what he asked. With the bag still secure across his shoulder, Allemand grabbed the end of the belt and pulled hard, causing Josey to lose her balance as the belt came out of the loops with a snap. She clung to the wall as she regained her footing.

"Hold your hands out in front of you," he ordered.

Unwilling to let him intimidate her, Josey lifted her steady hands up and forward. With the gun in one hand, Allemand took the belt with the other and awkwardly wrapped it around her hands, securing them together. The belt rubbed over some of her abrasions and caused her to wince.

"Okay, let's go," he ordered. Allemand led Josey down the hall toward a side exit.

—◆—

Back in the van, Jim picked up the conversation. He listened for a few moments. "Wait," he said to Brad and Mark. "Someone has Josey." He paused and listened. "He has a gun."

Brad wasted no time. He was already on his way back into the clinic. He had to get to Josey.

—◆—

As Josey was being pushed through the hall, she started to think. All the pieces were beginning to come together. "Now it all makes sense!" she explained. "Bobby!" She whirled around to face Allemand. "Bobby Cisco. He knew about your operation. He was following you. It was in his logbooks. Did you kill him?" Maybe she could distract him somehow.

"What difference does it make to you? You didn't even know the guy." Allemand spit the words out with contempt. He grabbed her again, forced her around, and pushed her forward.

"He was on to you," Josie continued. "Maybe he was about to tell the police. That accident. Someone called him in at the last minute to take that flight. That was you, wasn't it?" Josey struggled to buy time, hoping again that Brad was on his way.

"So what?" grumbled Allemand. "I didn't kill the guy. He was a psychopath, a loose cannon, and we're all lucky he's dead." He shoved her again. Allemand seemed to be getting some kind of sick pleasure out of manhandling Josey.

"It doesn't matter," she told him. "You're still a killer. I saw those dead bodies and those organs. How can you be involved in something so heinous?"

"Shut up or your organs will end up in one of those containers!"

— ✦ —

As Allemand continued shoving Josey toward the exit, he caught a glimpse of a man's form out of the corner of his eye. Holding on tightly to her arm, he quickly turned and pushed the gun hard into Josey's side.

— ✦ —

It was Brad.

"Drop your gun. Drop it!" Allemand ordered, his hands becoming a vise as he clamped into Josey's arm.

Brad carefully laid his gun on the floor and backed up.

Allemand, not releasing his firm grip on Josey, moved cautiously, not wavering. "Don't try anything. Okay. Here's the deal. I take it she's with you. I get out of here, and you get her back." Allemand was bargaining.

"Do you really think you can get away with this? We have enough evidence here to put you away for a long time—maybe even on a murder conviction. We have Big Vern. He's about to spill his guts," Brad said.

"I have nothing more to lose. My only hope of surviving this is to disappear. Trust me, I'll kill her!"

"What about Murillo?" Josey asked, surprised at her own bravery. "Do you really think he'll protect you? You won't be of any use to him anymore."

"Tell her to shut up or I'll use this gun on both of you," Allemand shouted. He looked like a madman, eyes glaring, nostrils flaring.

"Josey, enough!" Brad said.

Josey obeyed.

—✦—

Allemand was sweating profusely, and strands of his once-slicked-back hair were popping out in an unruly mess. "This shouldn't be happening," he said. "They said it was safe. No one would ever find out." He had never actually killed someone with his own hands.

—✦—

Brad could see that Allemand wasn't playing with them. He didn't want to take any chances with Josey's life. He slowly backed away, hands held up and apart. "Okay, okay. Just don't hurt her," Brad said, trying to distract Allemand so he could formulate a plan.

Allemand and Josey reached the exit. As he pushed her outside, she lost her footing and stumbled, falling on her already battered knees, causing one of her previous wounds to open. Blood seeped through her pants.

Allemand yanked her up, almost pulling her shoulder out of joint, and pushed her over to his black car, which was parked in the spot closest to the door. He pressed the button on the remote door opener. The car lights blinked, and a double beeping noise emitted from the vehicle. He opened the passenger door and ordered Josey to get in.

Josey complied. He slammed the door shut, almost catching her leg as she jerked it quickly into the car. She heard her door lock. He hurried around to the other side and got in, shut his door, and immediately hit the door lock button again. This time all locks were secured.

—✦—

As soon as Allemand and Josey were out of sight, Brad had run through the clinic, sliding dangerously on the polished tile floors as he rounded the corner to the exit. He headed for the shortest route to the van, which was still parked on a side street. Flying out the back door, Brad scaled over the fence and moved swiftly toward the van. During the drama at the clinic, Jim had kept the van motor running as he monitored communications. Words were unnecessary. After years of working with the others as a team, Jim had already jumped into the driver's seat and had the van rolling alongside Brad, who jumped in as though it was second nature. "Go around to the side of the building. Quick," Brad shouted. "We don't want to lose them!"

—✦—

Allemand put the car in gear and hit the gas. His car left tire marks as he raced off to the west on the barren roadway. He saw the van move in behind him. Leaning stiffly into the steering wheel, he pressed the gas pedal to the floor.

—✦—

Josey was surprised to hear a click—her door lock releasing.

Allemand abruptly yelled at her. "Open the door!"

"What!" she exclaimed.

"Open the door!"

"Are you nuts?"

He nudged her with the gun, proving how serious he was.

Although her hands were bound, her fingers were still flexible enough to grasp the door handle. Josey pulled on the latch. When the door was slightly ajar, Allemand slowed down and tried to push Josey out of the car. She struggled to remain in the car. But then her mind raced—gun—door? Finally deciding that the gun pointed at her was more dangerous than the potential pain of being hurled from the car, she picked the door. Instead of waiting to receive a final push from Allemand, she dove out of the car under her own power. She landed hard on the pavement. As she tried to roll as far away from the car as she could, she heard Allemand hit the accelerator and speed off.

—◆—

Brad, Mark, and Jim, following in the van, saw Josey tumble out of the car. Jim hit the brakes, swerving off to the left to avoid colliding with her body. The van screeched to a halt and stopped. Brad and Mark jumped down to the road and ran over to Josey as they watched Allemand's car fade off into the distance. Knowing it was too late to get back on his tail, Jim pulled the van over to the side of the deserted street, got out, and joined the others. Allemand had evaded them—for now.

Brad leaned over Josey. Her hands were still bound by her belt. She was awake but looked like someone had run over her with a lawn mower. She was covered with new scratches and cuts. "Josey!" Brad cried as he tried to see if she was conscious.

"I think I'm okay." A weak grin formed on her mouth as the words tumbled out.

Brad untied her hands while the other two men stood over them staring down at Josey.

"Gently, try to move your arms and legs," Brad said. She did as he asked—everything seemed to be working.

Brad helped Josey up, and they walked at a slow pace to the van. It was still dark, and the morning commuters had not yet hit the streets.

—◆—

"I'll be sore, but I'm okay." A wave of relief washed over her as she let Brad support her weight, his strong body a comfort. "He wasn't going that fast when he forced me out," she said. "I tucked my head in and tried to roll with the fall. I learned that from that self-defense course Cary made me take. I guess it finally paid off." Drawing in a ragged breath, Josey sighed. Brad hugged her and helped her into the van. "With all the accidents I've been having lately," she continued, "maybe I should start wearing protective padding everywhere I go." As she settled into the seat, she began to survey her new collection of bruises and scratches.

—◆—

Mark had already retrieved a first aid kit, and he quickly began to minister to her wounds.

"Allemand—he got away," Josey said, sounding disappointed.

"Don't worry, Josey," Brad said offering support. "We'll catch up with him. My guess is he'll try to get out of the country." At that moment he was more concerned about Josey's well-being.

"Then let's go to the airport," Josey replied. Brad realized she was trying to sound eager, but her weariness was all too evident to him.

"You're not going anywhere," Jim interjected as he started off toward the van. "We need to get you home."

Chapter 34

As the exhausted team drove back to Josey's house, Brad's cell phone rang, startling everyone in the van. It was Rene. It was nearly five in the morning. Brad frowned with concern as he handed the phone to Josey.

"Mom, Annie Cisco called again. She wants you to call her right away. She said it's about the airplane accidents. She sounded frantic— she said it was critical. It couldn't wait."

"Okay, what's her number? I'll call her now."

Josey dialed Annie's number and became all business.

"Oh, Ms. Cantwell. I should have told you this sooner. I tried calling you but you never called me back."

"I'm sorry, Annie—"

Interrupting Josey, Annie continued, "I told you Bobby was mad about something. Well, I lied at the deposition. I was afraid it would hurt my case. Bobby did go on some job interviews—at least five. Each one of the airlines turned him down. What really seemed to make him mad was that he said they were hiring guys with less experience than he had, and it wasn't fair. I was only worried about making sure our son, Robert, had a decent future. I didn't think it really mattered until now." Annie started to sob.

"It's okay, Annie. Take your time," said Josey, reassuring her.

"Okay, I'm all right." Annie sighed and Josey could hear her take a deep breath. "I found some letters addressed to Bobby. They're all from the airlines. They're all rejection letters."

"So Bobby was upset. We can appreciate that—who wouldn't be?" Josey said, thinking everyone gets upset when they get turned down.

"It's not that. There was a line drawn through one of the letters. And someone wrote a date and time at the bottom. It looks like Bobby's writing. I thought it was probably a date that he was going to follow up. There are times and dates at the bottom of the rest of the letters too."

"That's not unusual, Annie. Most applicants follow up even after being turned down," Josey commented.

"You don't understand," Annie said, sounding frustrated. "Three of the letters were from the airlines that recently had planes crash. The times and dates on the bottom of the pages match the crash dates."

"But Bobby's dead," Josey interjected, feeling a cold sensation creeping up her neck.

"Listen!" Annie's voice was suddenly firm. "The first crash happened before Bobby died and the next two happened after. Bobby must have set this up somehow in advance. He was pretty smart when it came to mechanics. He was capable of doing something like that." Annie began to cry. "Bobby was a psychopath. He was overbearing and possessive with me and little Robert. I couldn't get away from him. I only want to have a future for us now that he's dead." Annie continued, "One of the letters is from Viscount, and the date on it is today—six o'clock a.m." Annie was sobbing hysterically now. "You've got to do something. I'm so sorry." She sobbed again. "I'm so sorry!"

"Annie, this isn't your fault. We're so lucky you put the pieces together. You may be saving lives right now," Josey said as she tried to calm her down.

Annie gave her the rest of the information and hung up.

"What time is it?" Josey shouted to Brad with a little more strength. "We need to call Viscount right away. Get hold of the authorities and have them detain the six o'clock Viscount flight." The conversation with Annie Cisco had stimulated her adrenaline, and she had momentarily forgotten about her injuries.

Josey relayed Annie's story to the men in the van. They immediately made the calls to the FBI and TSA.

"We have time. Please, can we go to the airport?" Josey pleaded with Brad.

"Are you sure you're up to it?" Brad asked.

"Sure, my friend here"—she patted Mark on the shoulder—"fixed me right up!"

"We're on our way," said Jim. "Everybody buckled up?" He turned the van around and pressed down on the accelerator, throwing them all back into their seats. The five refuges sat quietly in the back not comprehending what was going on. They just stared at Mark.

"Don't worry. Right now there's a team getting the others out. They will be safe," Mark assured them.

Chapter 35

Allemand looked in his rearview mirror and watched the van swerve around Josey and stop. He continued down the road until the van was totally out of sight. He pulled over and dialed Murillo's number. "We have got to get out of town. They know about you too," Allemand said.

"That explains the concerns my airport security guard just relayed about suspicious people snooping around the hangar where my airplane is parked," Murillo said.

"There's a Viscount flight leaving for El Salvador at six this morning," said Allemand. "My bet is they'll think we'll leave on your private jet. It's unlikely that they'll expect us to be on that flight so soon. I don't have to reserve anything in advance. We can get on at the last minute, just before takeoff. I can get us on through the jet bridge, bypassing the terminal area. Meet me at the main Viscount hangar right away. We can get an airport vehicle and take it straight to the gate." Allemand realized the roles had changed—he was now the one in control, the one giving the orders.

Murillo had no alternative but to comply. He acknowledged Allemand with a grunt.

Murillo and Allemand arrived at the Viscount hangar within minutes of one another, and both rushed inside. Allemand showed the maintenance manager his badge. It wasn't necessary—the man knew him and escorted the two men to a utility cart that looked like a small jeep with the Viscount logo on the side.

"What gate is the six o'clock flight to San Salvador leaving from?" Allemand asked the manager.

"Gate twenty-six."

"Get in." Allemand motioned for Murillo to get into the cart.

Allemand took off. He drove the cart around the edge of the tarmac until he reached the Viscount gate area.

They saw the DC-8 parked at gate twenty-six and stopped beside the outside stairs that led up to the jet bridge.

Allemand and Murillo jumped out of the cart and ran up the stairs and through the door that opened at the end of bridge, next to the aircraft door.

Allemand flashed his badge to the flight attendant who was standing at the entrance to the cabin. He didn't need to demonstrate his authority; all his employees knew who he was.

"They're holding this flight," she told them. "We're just getting ready to offload the passengers. I don't know the details."

"Wait just a minute," Allemand ordered. The flight attendant hadn't reacted to his appearance at the gate, so no one must have called in to stop him from boarding. He had to act quickly before anyone knew he was there. "I just came from the maintenance hangar. Everything is fine," he said sternly.

The flight attendant wasn't about to argue with him. All of his employees knew his reputation.

"This man is with me," Allemand pointed to Murillo. "Find him a seat in first class."

Murillo left Allemand's side, brushed roughly past the flight attendant, and moved to the first-class cabin where he settled into a window seat.

Back at the front of the cabin, the attendant approached Allemand and said nervously, "Go on, check with the captain."

Allemand went into the cockpit and addressed the pilot, who was sitting in the left seat. The copilot sat watching. "I demand that you take off on time!" ordered Allemand.

"I've been instructed by my supervisor to hold the flight," countered the pilot.

"Are you questioning my authority?"

"I'm the captain of this flight, and I say we wait."

"And I am the vice president of this company, and I say we go as scheduled."

—✦—

The captain turned away. "Fine, but I'm not taking responsibility if anything goes wrong." He knew Allemand all too well. He also knew that it would do no good to argue with him. He summoned the flight attendant and told her to direct the gate agent to remove the jet bridge. The plane would be leaving on schedule.

"Flight attendants, prepare the cabin for take-off," the captain said over the PA system.

Allemand straightened his body, lifted his chin, and with a smug grin, moved back into the first-class cabin and sat down next to Murillo. They both sat in silence as the airplane taxied into take-off position.

Chapter 36

The van arrived at the airport a few minutes after six that morning. Jim pulled over to the curb in front of the terminal. Josey and Brad jumped out of the van and rushed to the Viscount counter, hoping that the flight had been canceled. They also hoped they'd be able to catch Allemand if he tried to board the plane.

"The flight to San Salvador, has it left?" Brad asked the ticket agent.

"No, we just found out the flight has been delayed. In fact, I think it might be canceled. We're still waiting to hear," the agent replied.

"What gate?"

"Gate twenty-six."

"Do you know if Mr. Allemand, your vice president, checked in for the flight?"

She typed something into the computer.

"No, I don't think so. His name isn't on the manifest."

Relieved, Brad grabbed Josey's hand, and they hurried through security and on to the gate to see if they could find anything suspicious about the flight.

They arrived at the gate to find the airplane gone. "What happened?" Brad asked the agent who was finishing up some paperwork.

"Apparently one of our vice presidents got on board and told the pilot that, whatever the problem was, it had been resolved," the agent said. "So the flight's just about to take off as scheduled."

"No!" Josey cried. "Call someone. Don't let it take off! There might be a bomb on board. Get the bomb squad, the police, and fire and rescue. Quick!" The agent just stared at her.

"Quick, Brad, we've got to get to the aircraft!" Josey said. She turned to the agent and flashed her NTSB card. That got his attention. "Can you get us a vehicle to get to the aircraft?"

The agent nodded and pointed to the jet bridge. "Go on down. There should be a cart at the bottom."

"What did you show him?" Brad said. "What made that agent jump so fast?"

Josey told him. "It was from my last visit.

It looked pretty official. I know you could have flashed one of your famous cards, but I wanted a turn this time." She winked.

Not wasting another moment, the agent called the tower and told them to stop the aircraft from taking off.

—✦—

Tower called the aircraft: "Viscount two-oh-six, abort, abort. There is evidence there might be an explosive on board."

The aircraft was still rolling down the runway.

"Copy that," the captain replied. "Aborting take-off. Where do you want us to go?"

"Don't go back to the gate," the tower said. "Taxi via Hotel to the Viscount hangar and hold out on the ramp for further instructions."

The captain did not say anything to alarm the passengers.

—✦—

It took a minute for Allemand to realize the aircraft was turning around. Once he did, he jumped up and ran to the cockpit door. He banged on the closed door. "What are you doing?" he screamed. "You need to get this flight in the air! Let me in!"

"Please, sir," said the flight attendant. "Take your seat. Everything will be fine." She took his arm, but he jerked it from her and kept banging on the door. He finally realized he was making a scene, and it would only hurt his chances of escape, so he quietly sat down.

—✦—

One of the other flight attendants answered the call from the cockpit. The captain told them to prepare for a quick egress from the aircraft through the passenger doors and jet stairs. They were not to engage the slides.

—✦—

The aircraft came to a stop surrounded by police cars, ambulances, and fire trucks. Police with bomb-sniffing dogs were preparing to enter the aircraft. The flight attendant opened the door to let the passengers out. The crowd was calm and quickly followed instructions to disembark.

Allemand looked at Murillo. "They don't know anything. This is just a coincidence. Just get off quietly and follow me."

As soon as the two of them stepped off the stairs, however, two large men grabbed their arms and pulled them aside. They immediately flashed their FBI cards. One of them said, "Gentlemen, you need to come with us. We are taking you in on numerous charges, including kidnapping and human trafficking." The other agent proceeded to tell them their rights.

Allemand and Murillo looked behind the agents to see Josey and Brad staring at them.

—✦—

Brad's phone rang. His face was intent as he listened to the voice on the other end. He hung up and stared at Josey.

"What?" Josey lifted her hand to her eyes to shade the rising sun.

"The body they found at the site of Bobby Cisco's accident wasn't Bobby."

Chapter 37

Early-morning strollers enjoyed the allure of the silky-blue waters of the Gulf of Mexico.

A man dressed in tropical attire, smoking a long, thin, brown cigarette with a gold stripe around the filter watched for an aircraft to arrive and take its final plunge into its deep dark grave. He flicked his ashes into the sand.

Bobby Cisco finally gave up watching the sky and slowly turned and walked away. He didn't like failure.

"It's not over yet."

Made in the USA
Monee, IL
29 February 2020